QUITE HONESTLY

Life couldn't be better for Lucinda Purefoy. Granted, it's a little embarrassing her father being the Bishop of Aldershot, but she's got a steady boyfriend, a degree in social sciences from Manchester University and the offer of a job in advertising. With all that, she feels she should 'pay back her debt to society' and 'do a little good in the world'.

To that end she joins SCRAP (short for Social Carers, Reformers and Praeceptors), an organization that trains girls like Lucy to become 'guide, philosopher and friend' to ex-convicts coming out of prison, to find them a job and home and to encourage them to kick the habit of stealing things.

And so Lucy finds herself standing outside the gates of Wormwood Scrubs, on a windy March morning, waiting to greet her first SCRAP 'client', a career-burglar called Terry Keegan. What happens next, after a short and hostile trip to Burger King, confounds expectations and produces a story full of surprises.

QUITE HONESTLY

John Mortimer

WINDSOR
PARAGON

First published 2005
by
Viking
This Large Print edition published 2006
by
BBC Audiobooks Ltd by arrangement with
Penguin Books Ltd

Hardcover ISBN: 1 4056 1326 2
ISBN 13:   978 1 405 61326 2
Softcover ISBN: 1 4056 1327 0
ISBN 13:   978 1 405 61327 9

British Library Cataloguing in Publication Data available

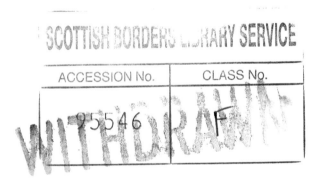
Printed and bound in Great Britain by
Antony Rowe Ltd., Chippenham, Wiltshire

For Kathy

'handy-dandy, which is the justice, which
is the thief?'

William Shakespeare, *King Lear*, Act 4, Scene 6

'Our interest's on the dangerous edge of things.
The honest thief, the tender murderer'

Robert Browning, 'Bishop Blougram's Apology'

1

I don't know why, but I've always wanted to do some sort of good in the world.

I used to have a boyfriend, Jason, who laughed at me and called me a 'do-gooder'. 'Meet my girlfriend, Lucy,' he would say. 'She's a do-gooder, of course.' And then he'd laugh. I don't know what he wanted—a 'do-badder'? A person who sets out to do one bad turn to somebody every day? No one wants that, surely? Anyway, I got tired of being called a 'do-gooder' and Jason and I split up, which I did regret, because I found him rather attractive and quite funny at times. But I didn't know why he was so irritated by my ambition to do a bit of good in the world.

I ought to introduce myself—I'm always called Lucy, but I was born Lucinda Purefoy. 'Purejoy' Jason used to call me when he was in a good mood. Oh, and I'd better tell you this right away. When I was young my father was a vicar in a big north London parish and Mum always said that he'd been spotted as having 'bishop potential'. This made Mum laugh, because she's more than a little irresponsible and tends to OD on gin and tonic before dinner. Although she had married one, she had little time for vicars, and even Dad agreed that some of the things they got up to at the General Synod showed naked ambition at its least attractive. Anyway, Mum was right and Dad got made the bishop of a large chunk of Surrey and Hampshire. He gets into the papers quite a lot because he can't see what's wrong with gay marriages, if that's what people want. He's extremely tolerant and told me I must make up my own mind about God. I have to admit that I haven't got round to doing it yet. Probably that's because I'm always kept pretty busy. I don't want to boast, but I did manage to get four decent A levels which took me to uni (Manchester), where I tended towards politics and sociology.

It was there I got interested in crime and the causes of crime, which I put down to poverty, a failing system of education and the values of the monetarist society which regards success as owning a four-wheel drive to take the children to school in and a second home in the Dordogne. At the time I hadn't even met a criminal.

After my degree, and work experience at the *Guardian*, when all my friends had gone off backpacking across Australia or thumbing lifts in Thailand, I really longed to do some good in the world, but I didn't necessarily want to go to Nepal or Cambodia to do it.

What I mean to say is I'd had a lot of privileges. Although my father being a bishop was more than a little embarrassing, I had, like I say, a secure and loving family. So I felt I had to repay my debt to society. But I really had no idea how to do it until I heard about 'praeceptors' and met Terry Keegan. Quite honestly, it wasn't until then that I found a real purpose in life.

I first heard about praeceptors from my friend Deirdre Bunnage. Deirdre was one of those irritating girls at school who were always telling you about their marvellous new boyfriends or the fact that they'd been asked to spend a long weekend in Acapulco with someone who'd been on television. Anyway, I hadn't long left uni when I bumped into her in the bar of the Close-Up Club in Soho. My then boyfriend, Tom, was very keen on getting into television so he joined the Close-Up and we went to hang out there in the hope of meeting someone in a television company who wanted to give Tom a job. Most of the people we met and talked to were also hanging out in the faint hope of meeting someone from a television company with a job to offer, so Tom wasn't getting very far. I was sitting with him at the bar, making a glass of white wine last a long time, when my old school friend Deirdre came over.

'I suppose your life seems pretty empty since you finished at Manchester,' she said. She was wearing that sort of surprised smile which I always found annoying. The fact that she was accompanied by someone she introduced as a 'well-known rap artist' added considerably to my irritation.

'It's not at all empty,' I told her, not altogether truthfully. 'Tom's going to give up market research and get a job with a television production company.'

'And *you*?' Deirdre was still smiling. 'You probably don't know what to do with yourself.'

I told her I'd had the offer of a PA job with an advertising agency, and I really wanted to do some sort of good in the world.

To my surprise, Deirdre's smile was no longer one of lofty disdain. She seemed genuinely delighted by my do-gooding intentions.

'That's wonderful, Lucy! You're a perfect candidate for SCRAP.'

'For what?' Her suggestion didn't sound entirely

complimentary.

'SCRAP. I've joined and it's fascinating work. You befriend young criminals fresh out of prison. Help them to lead an honest life. Make decent citizens out of them. You'd be perfect at it.'

'Why is it called SCRAP?'

'Social Carers, Reformers and Praeceptors. You know what a praeceptor is, don't you? Don't you remember any Latin from school? Anyway, we've got to go. Come on, Ishmael.' And with that, Deirdre went off with her rap artist, who turned out, in the fullness of time, not to be a rap artist at all.

And, in the fullness of time, I rang the office of SCRAP near to King's Cross Station on the off chance that I might be able to do some sort of good in the world.

*   *   *

'Why do they go on doing it? They've been to detention centres, youth custody, prison when they're seventeen or over. Put them inside for however long you want and they just come out and do it again! So they have to go back to prison, to their boredom and our considerable expense. Why can't they ever stop? Have you any ideas on the subject?'

'Poverty? Lack of education? The corruption of the monetarist society?' I remembered some of my essays from Manchester.

'No, none of that.' The large grey-haired man, with brown appealing eyes and a crumpled suit, swung gently in his office chair. He was Orlando Wathen, criminologist and chairman of SCRAP,

4

giving me the once-over when I applied to be a praeceptor. 'Some of these lads come from quite decent homes. They could hold down a reasonable job. What's so great about pinching laptops from the cars of sales reps who've stopped for a pee in a service station? There's a piece in here.' He searched among the books and pamphlets that littered his desk. 'Here it is! "Petty crime in the metropolitan environment". It's by a doctor. He suggests it's all because they take too much salt in their food. Seventy-five per cent of those convicted of theft in the Grimsby area admitted they liked their food well salted. Bloody nonsense! I take salt with my food and I don't steal laptops.' Mr Wathen looked up at me appealingly. 'Perhaps you'll discover what makes your customer pinch things.'

'I'll certainly try.'

'All our praeceptors say that, but they haven't enlightened me yet. I got your father's letter.' He searched and found it under a pile of pamphlets. 'He signs himself Robert Aldershot. That's not your name, is it, Miss Aldershot?'

'It's not his either. He signs like that because he's the Bishop of Aldershot.'

'Your father's a bishop?'

I had to admit it.

'We all have to rise above the unfortunate circumstances of our birth.' Mr Wathen was shaking with suppressed mirth. 'What's in a name anyway? My parents called me Orlando. No doubt they thought they'd produced a handsome wrestler who'd win the heart of the beautiful Rosalind. Instead of that they got a fat criminologist who's completely mystified by the causes of crime. You do realize, don't you, that your customers are

5

likely to resent you and refuse to cooperate?'

'Oh yes,' I told him, 'I'm expecting something like that.'

'Just as well.' Mr Wathen nodded energetically. At last he was certain of something. 'Expect the worst and you'll avoid disappointment.'

*   *   *

The one person who had no doubts at all about the causes of crime and the rising number of young criminals being locked up was SCRAP's chief executive, Gwendolen Gerdon. Gwenny, as everyone called her, was an oversized, blonde-haired, pink-cheeked woman, in her forties I suppose, who spoke in a high-pitched, rather breathless, little-girl's voice. She seemed to find crime and the causes of crime hugely entertaining. She never blamed the criminals we were meant to reform for any part of it. Instead she blamed the judges mostly and then the Home Secretary and the police for their unfair and unjust persecution of so many really quite harmless young men.

All the same, Gwenny was clearly the power behind the SCRAP office. She did the work while Orlando Wathen swung in his chair, speculating fruitlessly on the deeper causes of house-breaking, fraud and grievous bodily harm. It was Gwenny who organized our training sessions, every weekday evening for a month, after which I suppose we were meant to emerge as fully fledged, and reliable, praeceptors. We got talked to by prison officers, an assistant governor and someone who worked in prison education. But the one who depressed me most was a probation officer whom I was to come across again, not always happily, in the months to come. Mr Markby was generally of a sandy colour. He had sandy hair, a small sandy moustache and a dry, breathy sort of voice like the sound of wind over the desert.

'Just remember that you and the client [he meant ex-prisoner] aren't "friends",' Alexander Markby told us. 'You're his, or perhaps her, guide, philosopher and teacher. So don't offer him a cigarette, or he'll start to expect cigarettes all the time. Don't tell him what a good time you had at the pub the night before. That would put you on the same level. That's not right. You must never step down from your position as a teacher. Keep your distance.'

Rather surprisingly, Gwenny seemed to approve of the probation officer's advice. 'Take Alex's word for it and you won't go far wrong.' And she added, laughing, 'For heaven's sake, don't sleep with a client of either sex. We have had that happen in the past and it has always led to disastrous results. Keep in touch. That's the main thing. See that he's got a mobile and calls you morning and evening. First of all, see he's got somewhere to live and get him work. Make a nuisance of yourself until you get someone to give him a job—part-time if it has to be. Oh, and we'll want your full report at the end of each week. At the end of the course I'll meet you all individually and give you the names of your clients.'

On the final Monday morning, our little group of praeceptors posed with Orlando Wathen for a photograph on the steps of the SCRAP office. Then Gwenny told us who our prisoners were going to be. 'Alex Markby has suggested you for one of his very own clients,' she told me. 'He was impressed when I told him your father was a bishop and he said you might be able to give this chap a bit of moral backbone.' Not for the first time I cursed my father's choice of a job. What was moral backbone anyway, I wondered, and did I really have any of it to spare?

'The client's name is Terry Keegan.' Gwenny chuckled. 'He operated round the Ladbroke Grove area. Uncle almost in the big time, played a minor role in a Notting Hill Gate bank robbery. His grandmother lived round Bethnal Green and *she* can remember the Krays and the Richardsons!' She spoke of this family with a kind of awe, rather in the way some other sort of snob might discuss the relatives of a duke, or a movie buff might recall the great days of James Cagney and Greta Garbo.

'Terry began offending when he was about twelve. He was in a detention centre by the time he was fourteen.' Here again Gwenny spoke as though she was admiring the achievements of one so young. 'Last time he got four years for house-breaking from that bastard Judge Bullingham down at the Old Bailey. I have little doubt that he was stitched up by the police.'

'You mean he hadn't done the house-breaking?'

'Well, yes. I suppose he had.' Gwenny admitted it reluctantly and then added, 'But that doesn't alter the fact that Judge Bullingham's a bastard. You'll soon find out. The entire judicial system is completely hopeless. Anyway, Terry's coming out of the Scrubs on Thursday morning. He's been told to expect you. Orlando and I think it would be rather nice if you met him at the prison gates. He's got black hair, rather curly. Oh, and an unusually cheerful grin.'

So that's why I was waiting, at 8.30 a.m. on a wet March morning, outside the gates of Wormwood Scrubs for a young man with curly black hair and a cheerful grin.

Which is where this story begins.

2

A good many people down our end of Ladbroke Grove came from one-parent families. Sometimes I think, looking back on it, I came from a no-parent family.

After all these years I'm still not too sure who my dad is, and certainly Mum never told me. I always went by her name, which was Keegan, and it was only her family I ever met, so I reckon my dad was no more than a passing moment in her life.

What I remember most about Mum was when I was first at school—down in among the infants I was at the time—she would come and fetch me with this music stuck in her ears. You couldn't hold much of a conversation at home either because she liked her music loud. When I remember talking to Mum, it was all shouting over Duran Duran, at full volume.

I remember the kitchen where we lived on the estate, with plates stacked up by the sink sticking together, and I can remember wondering why there was so much washing-up because we weren't a big family. No dad, no brothers and sisters—just me. I suppose more got eaten because Mum often had guys she called my uncles around. Most of the time, of course, these uncles weren't uncles at all and then Mum would hustle me off to bed extra early and I'd lie awake listening to her *Music for Romantic Evenings* tapes played extra loud until they moved to the bedroom and I could get a bit of sleep. Anyway, I stayed with my mum and I put up with Duran Duran and her Romantic Evenings until one of the uncles turned out to be someone called Jack Levenhall, who gave it out that he owned a kebab place on Harrow Road. Much later, it turned out not only that he didn't own it, but that he'd been thrown out of it because of his habits. This Uncle Jack made it horribly plain that he fancied me more than he fancied my mum, so I moved out as quick as I could, and I never lived at her place after that.

Well, my mum knew where I was if she wanted to come after me, which she didn't. First I went to my gran's place in the Bethnal Green area, but she was always on about the big heavy villains she had known in her younger years, people like the Krays and the Richardsons and just how they could draw, with their razors, a perfect semicircle on the faces of those who disagreed with them. Gran seemed to admire this about the heavy men of her younger years, but hearing about it pissed me off, quite honestly, which is why I moved again and went to live with Aunt Dot in the buildings up near Kensal Rise cemetery.

Aunt Dot was the best. She was Mum's aunt, but a lot younger than Gran. She'd always talk to me without the incidental music, and it seemed like she always took an interest in me, and when I got into trouble and had to go away, Aunt Dot always seemed pleased enough to see me back. She had some of my mum's good looks, but in her they seemed softer and more appealing, that's what I thought at least.

Of course, my Aunt Dot was used to people going away for a while seeing as she was married to my Uncle Arthur. He was good to me also. He was

11

in a business way, out of anything I've ever attempted, robbing banks and building societies, threatening cashiers and customers with a shooter which he kept carefully cleaned and never even let me hold.

As you can imagine, this paid Uncle Arthur very well when he was working, and we used to go out to posh restaurants and even holidays in Spain. The trouble was he went away for a long time when things started going wrong, so we stayed on in the building in the Kensal Rise area, where the rent was reasonable, and Aunt Dot went off to the West End to do bits of cleaning, and that was when I was at school and Uncle Arthur was away from home.

It all started when I was about twelve. Something like that. This may surprise you, but I was quite a bright boy at school. For one thing I got the hang of the isosceles triangle long before anyone in the class understood it. It was at school I met Tiny McGrath. He wasn't called Tiny because he was especially small but to distinguish him from his very much older stepbrother, known as Chippy, not because he was a sort of carpenter but because of his huge appetite, at that time, for chips. He and Tiny had the same father but different mothers.

Chippy was always tall and in spite of what he ate he was quite skinny. He had a strange smile. I mean he only smiled with one side of his mouth. One side went up quite cheerfully while the other side stayed down as though it couldn't see the joke.

What I suppose he was was a natural leader; he had the gift of getting other people to work for him. He used to ask Tiny and me and some of our friends round to his place in Formosa Street and give us sweets or cigarettes, or a bit of money, to do little jobs for him. Such jobs, to be honest, usually consisted of stealing things, like pinching bottles of whisky and that from the off-licence while he kept the woman in charge amused with requests for crisps and sweets and other things she wasn't meant to sell, and she was busy explaining that we weren't entitled to be there anyway. All this led to us, but not Chippy, having to appear before the desk sergeant at the Paddington nick, where he told us that a life of crime would lead to misery and unhappiness. Looking back on it now, I'm still not sure that he was telling us the truth.

We graduated from there to car radios and the opening of car doors with a wire coat hanger. It was when I got caught at this that the friendly warnings stopped and I got seriously beaten up by members of the Metropolitan Police with time on their hands. After that I went inside for the first time as a Youth Offender.

It was after I left the Youth Offenders that Chippy and I got together seriously. We took to watching the smart houses in the Holland Park area, and noting when the milk and the papers were stopped because of the owners being away on holiday. We got skilled in the way of breaking and entering, and Chippy's cousin Ozzy Desmond had made a study of disconnecting burglar alarms. As I say, we did well enough, and I was about to give my Aunt Dot some of life's little luxuries when I got caught. I got four years from a judge who'd decided from the word go that I was a menace to society. Chippy, by the way, was in the getaway car near the house we got caught in, and he just drove off and left us to face the consequences.

13

So, it was then, when I was in real prison, that I decided I wouldn't get into no more trouble at all, and wouldn't get into fights. I kept myself to myself all those years. I'd get my meals and take them back to the cell and eat them on the table, which was, let's face it, the lid of the toilet. There was a lot of violence about at that time, from the London heavies, who the screws were afraid of. I saw one punch a screw in the chest during association, and the screw pretended not to notice it. He pretended it hadn't happened at all, he was just too frightened to make a point of it.

Well, you could quite often get into a fight in association, so I kept out of it. I stayed in my cell about twenty-three hours a day and I got used to it. I got so I didn't really want to be with other people. The time near the end of my sentence, when I was allowed days out with close relatives, I went out with my Aunt Dot, who told me Uncle Arthur had gone away again for ten years. She was always nice to me, my Aunt Dot, but I couldn't wait to get away from her. I wasn't listening to her hardly at all. All I could think of was how nice it would be to get to my cell for a bit of peace and quiet. So I asked her to take me back to prison early.

Of course, being alone so much, keeping out of everyone's way, I had time to read a lot of books. Most of them were a load of rubbish, crime stories, so called, by people who didn't know the first thing about crime.

Then I got a prison visitor called Simon who gave me a crime book by some Russian who suffered with epileptic fits. It was about murder and, of course, I never did a murder. In fact,

14

there's no violence in my record whatsoever. But I got stuck into this book and I found it interesting. Then I kept on getting called away for education classes, which taught me that three and three make six, a fact I already knew, and I lost the thread of the Russian book from time to time. But I persisted with the book whenever I could get away from education or watching further rubbish on TV during those dangerous moments of association. Simon got arrested for downloading pornographic material or some such affair, so for all I know he's somewhere inside the prison system, and I never saw him again.

I was all right reading in my cell. I mean, I was quite all right but I wouldn't have minded getting back into the fresh air, and by then I was able to work the system. We had ETS classes, which stood for Enhanced Thinking Studies. They asked you at the start what you were thinking and you had to say, 'I was thinking how great it'd be to go out on Saturday night and get pissed and hit someone's head with a hammer.'

If you said something like that, you started from a low point and your thinking could only improve you. So the ETS person gave you a good report, which helped towards parole.

Then I began to get visits from a woman who asked me to call her Gwenny and said she was from an outfit called SCRAP. One time she came, she told me the whole prison system was rotten and all prisons needed blowing up. This worried me and I began to wonder if this SCRAP was some sort of terrorist organization. But then she asked if I'd like SCRAP to fix up for some sort of person to look after me when I got out and help me to lead

15

an honest life. Then I realized that SCRAP was another of those things, like ETS. It was better to go along with it if you wanted to leave the Scrubs as quick as possible.

This got a bit delayed, however, by my probation officer, Mr Markby, who gave me an interview when the question of parole came up. He said that I was extremely intelligent (ha ha) and that I knew exactly the right answers to give (which I did) but that I didn't seriously mean them (which perhaps I didn't) so I should stay inside because I couldn't be trusted. Which was why I didn't get parole. It just shows that I wasn't as good at working the system as I thought I was.

Anyway, this incident made me very suspicious of probation officers and all suchlike who say they're only trying to help you and support you, when what they're really after is to keep you inside for quite a bit longer. All the same I felt relieved, because, quite honestly, I wasn't ready to face the outside at that particular moment in time and I had to finish the Russian book, which I was able to do before my eventual release.

One week before I got out, I got a visit from the chaplain, who said that SCRAP had found a praeceptor, whatever that might mean, Lucinda Purefoy. She was an excellent choice seeing that her father was a well-known bishop. I smiled at him, of course, and seemed to agree but I'd already decided, once I got out, not to have much more to do with probation officers and SCRAP women who could no doubt turn the way Mr Markby did. Being out of prison means that you're free, doesn't it? At least that's the way I looked at it at the time.

*   *   *

They were a bit slow at the office that morning. They gave me the clothes back I was wearing when I got arrested. The sweater I had was all moth-eaten but they said they could do nothing about it. I got £46.75 and a travel warrant and then they opened the gate and I was out in the rain.

I hadn't taken more than a couple of gulps of fresh air when this girl came towards me, all smiling. She was wearing black trousers, a long overcoat and a white shirt. It looked as if she'd dressed up for the occasion. Now I'm not sure why that annoyed me so much.

Which is where this story begins.

3

He had dark curly hair and what I think they call 'prison pallor'. What he didn't have was a cheerful grin. Quite honestly, when he caught sight of me he looked distinctly uncheerful. All the same I managed a big smile as I moved towards him. Probably I was breaking Mr Markby's number one rule and looking too friendly. But what the hell, I had to form some sort of relationship, even if he was going to be my pupil.

'Hi there!' I said. 'You must be Terry Keegan.'

He stood looking at me in silence. To be truthful, he seemed astonished, as though he'd been unexpectedly approached by some sort of lunatic. Eventually, he spoke.

'What if my name's Terry Keegan? What do you want to make out of it, man?' He spoke in a low gruff voice which came as an unpleasant surprise in the cheerful chap I'd been instructed to meet.

'I don't want to make anything of it. And I'm not a man, actually.' I thought this was quite a funny thing to say, all things considered. Anyway I laughed, but Terry certainly didn't. 'I'm sure SCRAP have warned you about me, haven't they? I'm your praeceptor. Probably you don't know what that means.'

'You needn't bother to tell me.'

'It means I'm your guide and philosopher.' In deference to Mr Markby, I failed to say friend. 'I'm here to help you find a job, a place to live and that sort of thing. Support you in any way I can. And I'm here to see you don't ever go back inside that place again.'

The going-to-work traffic had grown louder and heavier rain was splattering the pavement. I had to raise my voice to be heard as I said the last sentence very loudly, so a small party of girls on their way to school turned their heads to stare curiously at Terry. This caused him to look even more crossly at me.

'I don't need no help,' he growled, 'so fuck off, will you?'

Well, I had to look on the bright side. At least he'd stopped calling me 'man'.

'My name's Lucinda Purefoy,' I told him, 'but that's a bit of a mouthful, so it's perfectly all right if you call me Lucy.'

'I don't need to call you anything. In fact I don't need you, full stop. So I'm fucking off, thank you very much.'

'Don't lose your temper with your client. Never give him that particular satisfaction.' I was finding Mr Markby's instructions particularly hard to follow. All I could think of doing was to look my client full in the eyes and say very deliberately, 'Well then, fuck you!'

The effect of this was surprising. First Terry looked at me and seemed deeply shocked and even silenced. Had I said that in front of my father, the tolerant bishop, he wouldn't have batted a single eyelid. Terry Keegan, with a string of convictions as long as your arm, was far more easily shocked. In fact he said, 'What do you mean?' which seemed to me to be a completely pointless question.

'I mean I've been training for a month listening to dull lectures. I've postponed a job with an almost decent salary in an advertising agency. I'm prepared to spend time away from my boyfriend, Tom, who's good-looking, never swears at me, has a perfectly clean record and is going to end up with an important job in television. And I've done all that to help you.'

'I don't need no help!' He was still angry.

'Oh yes, you do. Don't you understand? Eighty-five per cent of criminals reoffend within two years of their release from prison. If I take my eye off you you'll be back pinching laptops on garage forecourts or whatever you used to do.'

'Breaking and entering premises by night.' It seemed I had insulted him by talking about the laptops and he had a more important crime to boast about.

'All right then. Breaking and entering. Whatever. Now tell me what you want to do that's free and legal and has nothing to do with sex and we'll do it.'

He stood there, looking at me in silent thought—I'm sure it wasn't silent prayer—and then he said, rather improbably, 'Burger King.'

'What?'

'I've had Scrubs food for nearly three years. I want to go to Burger King.'

'All right,' I said, and I waved, I'm afraid rather desperately, at a passing taxi. Talk about extravagance. I'd already broken practically every rule that Mr Markby had ever given us.

*   *   *

In the Burger King, Terry's behaviour improved slightly, which wasn't hard considering it was starting from such a remarkably low level. I bought him a Whopper burger with fries and onion rings and a big milky coffee with five spoonfuls of sugar. After he'd finished that, he ordered another Whopper and I'm sorry, Mr Markby, but I paid for all this because I couldn't stand any further argument. I know it was weak of me.

As he finished the second Whopper I thought, poor sod, he'll become disgustingly fat and lose any attractiveness he might have to women. I wondered if I should warn him of this, but then decided that I couldn't be bothered. Instead I went on to more important business.

'I have to make sure you've got a mobile phone.'

'You want to give me a few minutes to pinch one?' He gave me his first grin, but I decided it was high time to become strict and stand no more nonsense.

'Of course not. I've bought you one to save you getting into trouble.'

I gave him the phone I had paid for, although my instructions from Mr Markby were simply 'to make sure the client had a mobile'. It might have been very thick of me, but I couldn't think of any way I could be sure of that without buying the thing.

'Does it take photographs?' Terry was turning over the little machine and looking at it critically.

'No, it doesn't take photographs. And you've got to ring me on that every morning and at six o'clock every evening so I know how you're getting on. Is that understood?'

'Yes, man,' he gave me a sort of mock salute, 'if that's your orders.'

'Never mind about my orders. Now, your

21

probation officer tells me he's got you a place in a hostel.'

'No.'

'No, he hasn't got you a place?'

'No, I'm not going to no hostel.'

'Why not?'

'Because I'm free now, aren't I? I can live my own life. I don't have to spend another night in no sort of prison place Mr Markby's sent me to. Forget it, man.'

The worst of it was that I could see his point. That's my greatest weakness, being able to see other people's points.

'All right,' I said, 'where do you want to go?'

'My Aunt Dot's.'

'Where's your Aunt Dot live?'

'Buildings up the end of Ladbroke Grove. Kensal Rise area. She's always been pretty good to me, my Aunt Dot.'

I looked at him. He seemed to mean what he said. Once again I disobeyed instructions. 'OK then. But call me on your phone as soon as you settle in. I'll try and smooth it out with Mr Markby.'

Terry, it seemed, thought it over, wiped his mouth on the napkin provided and stood up. 'I'll be getting along then.'

'I don't suppose you'll say "thank you".'

'Thank you for what?'

'Taxi here, two Whoppers with fries and onions, and letting you choose your accommodation.'

'I never asked you to do any of that,' he said, and he sounded serious. 'It was you did all the asking.'

4

'You must be Terry Keegan.'

That's what she said to me. Right out. The first thing. All smiles she was as she crossed Du Cane Road to get to me just when I heard the small door in the gate shut behind me. Well, she was right. I had to be Terry Keegan, and I didn't want her or anything about her.

You know what I felt when she came up to me? Like I was being arrested all over again.

All right. I'd done nearly three years. I'd had my parole delayed by one of her lot, Mr Markby, the probation officer. I'd kept my head down and read *Crime and Punishment*. I'd done my best to say the right things to the right people all that time. Now all I wanted was to be free of the whole lot of them.

I wanted to breathe a bit of fresh, free air that didn't smell of toilets and disinfectant and stale food and men's bodies. I wanted to decide what I was going to do for a change and not leave it to other people. I wanted to be shot of all those concerned-looking individuals who thought they knew more about Terry Keegan than Terry Keegan knew about himself.

And there was one of them waiting for me, on the other side of Du Cane Road, the very moment I got out.

I'd worked out a way of dealing with her, of course. I remember how Chippy McGrath used to put off girls he thought were getting too friendly, or that he wanted to get rid of. He used the expression 'Fuck you, man' as almost his only way of communication with such people, and the result was that they didn't hang about near him for very long.

So when this one came on to me with all that bright 'let's be friends' kind of chatter, I gave her the full McGrath, delivered with his special sort of grunt.

What worried me was that it didn't seem to have any effect on her whatever. Talk about persistent! What worried me even more was that she swore back at me. I don't like to hear a woman swear. It reminds me of my mum and seems to go against the laws of nature, like women getting drunk. My Aunt Dot wouldn't do either of those things and I didn't see why this girl, who took it on herself to improve me, had to swear like Chippy McGrath.

Well, I knew we'd never get on with each other after that event. But there was one thing she could do for me. I still felt the old prison hunger for a decent bit of food that could fill you right up, and I didn't want to break into my £46.75. Not that soon anyway. So I expressed my need for a Whopper with fries and onions. I thought that might work with her. She could help a poor, hungry criminal without me ever having to see her again.

Can you believe this? She put up her finger for a taxi. We could have gone to the bus stop or down the tube. No. She was a woman who used bad language and rode around in taxis. Showing off was what I put it down to.

Anyway, I bet we were about the only customers to arrive at Burger King in Notting Hill Gate by taxi. And when I'd polished off a Whopper with all of what comes with it and was well assured that I wouldn't have to burrow into my £46.75, I felt a lot calmer.

What I remember most about that time at the Burger King was that I got given a mobile phone. Of course I'd had phones, and plenty of them, but not ones that were given up voluntarily. And what I remember thinking was, this is rather dull, being given a mobile without the interest attached to stealing it. She told me her number was in the phone and I should call her every morning and evening, which I hadn't the slightest intention of so doing.

One thing she did do was to agree to me going to Aunt Dot's and not to any more prison-like accommodation in any hostel. She said she'd deal with Mr Markby about where I lived and I suppose, looking back on it, I should have said thank you for that, because I had no wish to deal with Mr Markby on any point, particularly on the subject of where I lived.

At the end of the meal, she said I ought to thank her for the Whoppers and dealing with Mr Markby. What I said, and I remember this clearly, was I hadn't asked her to do anything for me, and it was her who was doing all the asking.

Well, that was true, wasn't it?

*   *   *

'Old lady no longer live here.'
'Why, where's she gone?'
'Old lady dead.'
When we parted, my teacher, lecturer, whatever she was, had given up taxis. She reminded me to phone or text her when I was settled in. So I'd

25

walked up to the far end of Ladbroke Grove so as not to disturb my £46.75 and turned off towards Kensal Rise cemetery. The high tower block looked only a little more inviting because some graffiti artist had decorated its lower walls with a pattern of hearts entwined together, and I got out at the tenth floor and walked along the concrete balcony.

The place seemed quieter than usual. Of course it was only about ten o'clock in the morning but I could hear no nicked cars racing around the block, not even quarrels or the occasional scream, like there usually was when I got home, not to mention the odd shot. Some kids were playing football that ought to have been in school. All the same, the buildings had never seemed quieter than when I opened Aunt Dot's flat with the keys they'd given me back in the Scrubs that morning.

I opened the door and let loose a great burst of Chinese voices. I don't know what they thought. Probably that I'd come to rob them, because I didn't ring the bell. But there were so many of them, at least three or four men, one of them picked up a baseball bat, three or four women, some small children and a baby who screamed at me.

It wasn't until I'd quietened them down and explained who I was that they told me. The old woman was dead. My Aunt Dot had passed over.

And Uncle Arthur? I didn't need to be told where my Uncle Arthur was. Gone away. No doubt after some bungled robbery or other. That was the trouble with prison. They never told you anything. Aunt Dot had died and there was I, alone in my cell, reading the Russian book and not knowing

26

anything about it.

When I was leaving the buildings, I have to say I felt really lonely. More lonely even than I'd ever felt inside. It suddenly struck me, I'd stepped out of prison into nothing at all. And I didn't have any idea what I was going to do next.

What I did next, I suppose, only went to show how unfit I was for the real world outside the Scrubs. I wandered about round London. I'd made up my mind not to go to the hostel. I wasn't going to give Mr Markby the satisfaction. So when I left the buildings, the whole day stretched in front of me like a long sentence. The worst was that I had no idea where I was going to serve it.

I'd walked back into London as far as Bayswater when I had the idea of phoning Chippy McGrath.

'You're out! In the land of the free. I'll buy you a drink!' That was what Chippy said when I got to him through the small army of protectors, minders and hangers-on that seemed to be around him in his place, what the ever-popular Chippy called 'a maisonette property off the Edgware Road'.

'I need a bit more than a drink, Chippy,' I had to tell him. 'Would you mind if I kipped down at your place? Just till I can get something fixed up.'

'No problem. Meet you for that drink and we'll fix it all up.'

'Where's the drink?'

'Beau Brummell Club.'

'Where the hell's that?'

'Harrowby Street. Bright lights, big bouncers in the doorway, you can't miss it.' And my old school friend rang off to attend to more important business.

Well, at least I've got friends, I thought. But it

was a long time till six o'clock. Life out of prison seemed to leave you with a lot of hours to fill in.

Anyway, I invested in cigarettes and a toothbrush and toothpaste plus an evening paper and a packet of sandwiches from Marks which I took to a bench in Regent's Park. The rain had stopped but there was a sky like a grey prison blanket all over the lake, so I sat there reading the paper and feeding bits of my sandwich to the ducks. By this time, my wealth was down to £36.

*   *   *

'So you're out! We can work together again.'

'No, I don't think so.'

'Why ever not? We done some good jobs together.'

'I'm not too keen on going back inside.'

'So what're you going to do?' Chippy had changed over the time I'd been away. He looked older, but he was much smoother. No longer the Chippy who'd say 'Fuck off, man' to any woman. He had the self-satisfied smile of a successful person.

'I suppose get some sort of job,' I told him, a bit uncertainly.

'What sort of a job? Not much use with your convictions.' Chippy spoke from a lofty height, as though he had the cleanest character ever, which was far from the truth. 'You work along with me, Terry, and you could live like me.' Here he waved his hand round the Beau Brummell Club as though he owned the whole place. There were tables with girls with dickie bows round their bare necks and naked shoulders who were dealing out cards and raking in money. Some of them spun wheels and raked in even more money. There were fruit machines clattering round the walls. In and out of the shadows round the bar there were easy-to-come-by women and men straining the buttons on their dark suits. I heard a few posh voices piping excitedly away and I thought, this is where the tip-top people come to mix with the crims.

Chippy himself was perched on a high bar stool staring at what seemed to be his personal bottle of champagne. Give him the credit, he poured me a glass without hesitation.

'Bubbles, Terry. I bet you didn't get many of them in the Scrubs.'

'Too right,' I agreed.

'You ought never to have got caught on that last job, Terry.'

We'd made sure the couple who owned the house were away on holiday. It was just our luck they'd left a key with their daughter. She arrived with a pack of beefy young men just as I was packing up the last of the silver! Chippy, of course, heard their arrival and escaped in the getaway car. My friend Chippy, you'll have noticed, always managed to escape.

'It was a bit careless of you, Terry, to choose that particular gaff. I was lucky to get away.'

'Of course. You're always lucky. When you get nicked you'll have had no previous convictions.'

'What do you mean "when I get nicked"? I'm a law-abiding citizen, Terry. Let me give you one of these.' At which he produced a wallet and extracted a business card which read 'Leonard McGrath, BSc. Financial Adviser. Environmentally Friendly Investments. Mortgages and Home Loans

Negotiated' and gave the address of his maisonette in Connaught Square. I had to burst out laughing.

'What's so funny?'

'Leonard. I always knew you as Chippy. Are you really a Leonard?'

'Of course I am.'

'And what's all this BSc?'

'Bachelor of Science.'

'Are you one of those?'

'Of course I'm not. Anyway, as I say, it was careless of you, Terry, to get us into that particular house. You bloody nearly lost my good character for me. I can't take you out for a job if you're going to be careless.'

I explained again that I'd finished with that side of life and all I wanted was somewhere to kip down for the night until I could make other arrangements. Could Chippy help?

'I don't see why we shouldn't fit you into a corner of the maisonette.' It was then that there was a burst of music from his top pocket and he got deep into a conversation to which he contributed nothing much more than a number of grunts. As soon as he'd put his phone back in his pocket he stood up. 'Sorry, my lad, got to go. Urgent business. Oh, and the maisonette's going to be chock-full, so you'll have to make other arrangements. But do finish the bottle.'

Then Chippy was gone. I wasn't too upset, because I knew I had enough for a room for a couple of nights at least. So I took no notice when my phone rang and I knew it was Lucy, and when she texted me to ring her urgently I certainly didn't feel the need to reply.

And then my first day of freedom began to fall

apart. Just after I'd knocked back the last glass, the barman asked me for money, saying my friend had been in a hurry and said he'd leave me to settle up. This led to a series of arguments which I needn't go into, ending up with an invitation to step into the manager's office for the opportunity to discuss how expert the chuckers-out from the front door were at beating up customers who didn't meet their obligations. That was when I parted with £36, apparently the price of a bottle of bubbles at the Beau Brummell Club, so my remaining capital was nil.

With the prospect of a decent bed for the night fading away, and still determined not to surrender to Mr Markby and his prison hostel, I thought I'd try and do what had worked for me a time or two when I was a teenager, which was to head off to the super-loo on Euston Station.

It wasn't bad in there, with a few creature comforts such as showers, and I still felt able to ignore Lucy ringing my phone. However, there was a bloke in that super-loo, where such blokes do gather, who was giving me the sort of looks my mum's boyfriend was so free and easy with, and which was among the reasons for me leaving home. I didn't want to get into trouble fighting on my first night out, not in the super-loo or anywhere else come to that. So I moved to my last known address for that night, which was a bench on platform four, which I had entirely to myself from around ten o'clock. I went to sleep soon after Lucy's last unanswered call.

I woke up with a mouth like the floor of a parrot's cage, stiff legs and bitter thoughts about the superior comfort of my single cell in the

Scrubs. Some unseen visitor must have visited my bench when I was asleep and made use of the opportunity for a good vomit. In the distance the trains were clanking into position. When my phone rang at 6.48 I gave up the fight and answered it.

'Terry Keegan speaking.' I tried to sound self-confident and successful.

'Where on earth are you?'

'Honeymoon suite. The Ritz Hotel.'

'You're not!'

'Of course I'm bloody not.'

'Are you at your Aunt Dot's?'

'I couldn't stay at Aunt Dot's.'

'Why not?'

'It wasn't convenient for her.' I didn't want to tell her the truth and have her feeling sorry for me.

'So where did you sleep?'

'Not a bad bench. Handy for platform four at Euston.'

'And why didn't you ring me? I rang you. I texted you. Why didn't you answer?'

'I thought I could manage on my own.'

'You obviously can't. Why didn't you get a room somewhere? You've got money.'

'Not now I haven't.'

'What did you do with it?'

'Spent it all on a bottle of champagne.'

'You're joking!'

'I wish I was.'

She was quiet then and I wondered if she was going to cut off on me. Oddly enough, and for the first time, I hoped she wouldn't.

She didn't.

'One last chance,' she said. 'Get yourself over to Waterloo.'

'Where?'

'Waterloo Station. Meet you by W. H. Smith's at, let's say, 8.30. I'm telling you, it's your last chance.'

5

'It was you did all the asking.' That was what he actually said to me, remember? After I'd shelled out from the not much money I'd accumulated from waitressing over the Christmas period. I told him straight out, again if you remember, I reminded him that I'd bought him a mobile and second helpings at the Burger King and taken my courage in both hands and rung his probation officer to get him out of staying in the hostel. I'd done all that and all he could find to say was, 'It was you did all the asking.'

It was as if he expected me to go down on my knees and thank him for allowing me to spend out on him. Is that the trouble with trying to do a bit of good in the world? There are a lot of people in the world who don't really want any good to be done for them. So they'll never thank you for it.

You can tell how disappointed I felt with this doing-good business. After he'd failed to answer my calls all day and all the evening, I decided to ring the advertising agency and tell them I'd be able to start work next week.

It was when I'd been kept awake all night with anger and frustration I decided to give him the chance of one last call. Miracle of miracles, he answered me.

All the same, he sounded quite patronizing, as though he was too busy to be bothered with telephone calls. Too busy sleeping on a bench in Euston Station! And he told me he'd spent all his prison money on a bottle of champagne. You know what that was, don't you? That was a cry for help.

All right. It's a bit of a thankless task doing any sort of good in the world, but if you ever set out to do such a thing you can't simply ignore them, not cries for help. That was when I told him to be at W. H. Smith's on Waterloo Station, to which he'd no doubt have to walk if he'd spent all his money on champagne, and serve him damn well right.

If he wasn't there that would be a definite end to my trying to do good in the world. But before I met him I had to speak to my father.

*   *   *

'You're here then.' I looked at Terry in amazement. I'd said 8.30 and I'd got to W. H. Smith's on Waterloo Station at exactly 8.40. And there he was, looking a bit tired certainly, but alive and apparently unrepentant.

'I've been buying you a ticket,' I told him. 'And it's about the last thing I'm buying you if you don't remember to phone me every night and every morning. I'm very disappointed in you, Terry.' I was beginning to realize you can't do good to people without being quite nasty to them occasionally.

'All right then. Where are we going?'

'To visit my parents.'

'Oh yes.' He seemed determined not to show any sign of surprise. 'Where do they live then?'

'Not very far. Aldershot.'

'No, I mean what they got? A house or just a maisonette?'

'As a matter of fact it's a palace,' I said truthfully. At which I clearly succeeded in surprising Terry.

'Pull the other one,' he said, 'it's got fucking bells on it!'

*   *   *

My dad is very handsome for a bishop, or indeed for anyone. He has chiselled features, clean cut, regular. His hair is going grey, in rather an attractive manner. He keeps thin by riding for miles uphill on a stationary bike he has fixed up in the bathroom. He wears the thinnest of dog collars and a pectoral cross said to have formed part of the pulpit where Archbishop Cranmer preached a sermon—although I'm not sure that the ecclesiastical outfitter wasn't having Robert on a bit there. (My father always encouraged me to call him 'Robert' and not 'Dad', just as I had to call my mum 'Sylvia'.)

When I collared him in the bathroom, and found him panting a bit to get up the hill, he was wearing black socks, a quite flattering pair of Gucci underpants and a T-shirt he'd bought as a joke when he was in San Francisco at an Episcopalian congress. This garment had written across the chest the words 'Skanky Danky'. I'm not sure that my dad had any idea of what those words meant. He was, as always, very clean from the bath, but he'd not yet applied his daily squirt of Tommy Tingle's Fragrance for Men.

As a Christian, my dad was, I thought, an expert at doing good in the world, and he'd already shown considerable interest in the Terry Keegan story, so I gave him an update. As a professional forgiver of trespasses, he seemed to take Terry's appalling

36

behaviour less seriously than I did.

'Sounds a bit of a character,' he said. 'Still with the possibility of redemption.'

'He spent all his money on a bottle of champagne.' Here I was giving Terry the benefit of the doubt. 'I thought it might be a cry for help.'

'Or just a cry for champagne.'

My dad smiled and got off his bike, which buzzed in a complaining manner until he switched it off. Then I told him we had to have a last-chance plan for Terry. And once I told him that, Dad became extremely helpful.

*   *   *

The Bishop's Palace at Aldershot isn't really all that palatial. It's old, draughty and covered with ivy. To me, it always seems to have the smell of Sunday lunch, to which my dad invited whoever had preached that morning in the cathedral, and at which my mum was inclined to close her eyes and drift off into a snatch of sleep, having been in charge of the pre-lunch cocktails. That morning my dad greeted Terry as though he were some strange and wonderful being from outer space.

'Do sit down, Mr Keegan. That's really the best chair, near the window, if it's not too draughty for you. Darling, wouldn't Mr Keegan like a biscuit with his coffee?'

'Or something a little stronger than coffee?' Mum was looking longingly at the trolley with the gin bottle on it.

'Too early.' Robert was unusually decisive. 'Far too early for anything of that nature, wouldn't you agree, Mr Keegan?'

37

'He answers to the name of Terry,' I told them.

'Terry. Yes, of course, Terry. Coffee all right for you, is it, Terry?' Here Robert stood up to offer Terry a biscuit, which he took in silence. This silence continued while Dad resumed his seat and went on in the friendliest way possible.

'Well then, Terry. Lucy's told us you're just out of bird?'

'Out of what?' Terry seemed genuinely puzzled.

'Porridge. The nick. The cooler. Chokey. Whatever you call it.'

'I call it prison.' Terry wasn't giving my father any marks for trying.

'Ah yes, prison—of course. Well, Lucy tells us you're just out of prison.'

'Yesterday.'

'What?'

'I got out yesterday.'

'Well, that must have come as a great relief to you. I'm only sorry you didn't have better weather for it.' My heart went out to Dad, who was clearly growing desperate.

'I don't care about the weather,' Terry told him.

'No, I don't suppose you saw much of it in prison, did you?'

'Not a lot, no.' For the first time, Terry allowed himself to smile, and I was, perhaps unnecessarily, grateful to him.

'Not a lot, as you say, Terry. So amusingly.' Dad smiled back. 'And what exactly were you in prison for, if it's not a rude question? Lost your temper, did you? Had a moment of blind rage and stabbed someone? I had a curate when I was a vicar in Deptford. He just went berserk one night and stabbed a really lovely woman who was training to

38

become a priest.'

'I've got no violence on my record.'

'Well done, Terry! Terribly well done. They sent my curate to Broadmoor, I remember. That's not really prison, is it?'

'No, it's where they put the loonies.'

'And you're not one of those, are you, Terry? You certainly are not. So what was it? Drugs? They seem to be the usual thing nowadays.'

'I never done drugs. Can't understand what's the attraction. Those that do it, I'd lock them up and throw away the key.'

'Oh, I'm not so sure about that.' Dad seemed shocked at Terry's intolerance of crime. 'People commit far worse crimes under the influence of drink, so I'm given to understand.' Here he kept a steady eye on Mum and the gin bottle. 'Was it perhaps sex with someone under the age of consent?'

'That's disgusting!' Terry seemed in real danger of losing his temper. But Dad continued to smile.

'So what was it that got you into trouble—what was your *specialité de la maison*?'

'My what?'

'What particular brand of expertise landed you in chokey?'

I saw no particular future in this conversation, so I supplied the answer. 'Terry's *specialité*, if you *have* to call it that, was breaking into houses at night and stealing stuff. Terry was a thief.'

'Ah,' Dad nodded, still smiling, 'a blagger. Now I understand. That's good.'

'You don't mean that, do you?' Terry seemed profoundly shocked.

'What?' Dad looked puzzled.

'You don't mean that it's good at all, you think it's very bad, don't you? It's what they teach you in church. If you do it, you'll go down to hell.'

'Hell?' Dad looked puzzled again, as though Terry were speaking a foreign language, or at least referring to matters with which he was no longer familiar. 'What do you mean by that exactly?'

'You know.' Terry looked surprised at my father's ignorance, but patient with it. 'Hell, the place you go to after you're dead. Lots of big fires and devils there with red-hot forks to torment you.'

'Oh dear me.' My father was trying hard to stop himself laughing. 'Whatever gave you that idea?'

'Friend of mine in Feltham Young Offenders. His father knew about it from someone in the Salvation Army.'

'Well, I'm afraid your friend from Feltham Young Offenders and his father and the Salvation Army are seriously out of date. We don't believe in devils with red-hot toasting forks any more.'

'So you think it's all right then?'

'I think what's all right?'

'Thieving. And that.'

'No, no.' My father was now laughing openly. 'Of course it's not all right. But we must always try to understand.'

'Understand why people nick things?' I was pleased, in a way, that Terry and Dad seemed to have struck up a conversation which at least caused Terry to say more to him than he ever had to me. I was only a little worried because Terry, as he spoke, was looking with particular interest at the silver loving cup on the mantelpiece which had been presented to Dad when he left his

40

London parish.

'I suppose,' my father said, 'it all comes down to poverty. Poverty makes you steal.'

'We didn't have poverty.' Terry seemed rather offended by the suggestion.

'Did you not? How curious.'

'My Uncle Arthur brought home a pretty good wage, when he was in business. Not when he was away, of course. And Aunt Dot went up the West End, charring for a smart set of people, until she passed over.'

'How extremely interesting.' It was Dad's great talent to appear interested in the most unlikely conversations that had, I thought, led to his promotion in the Church. 'And what was your Uncle Arthur's job exactly?'

'Job? Jobs. He did banks, building societies. All sorts of offices.'

'You mean he worked in them?'

For the first time since I'd known him, Terry laughed. Dad, with his remarkable talent for getting on with people, had actually amused him. 'No. I mean breaking into them. Not always successful, Uncle Arthur. That's why he was away a good deal.'

'Yes, of course.' Dad seemed to be getting out of his depth. 'Of course he would have been.'

'However many times he was away,' Terry assured him, 'he looked after us, Aunt Dot and me.'

'Well, that must have been a great consolation to him.' Dad retreated into clerical solemnity. 'Well, we must have a long talk about all that sort of thing. Remember, my door is always open. Now, down to business. Lucy tells us you've been

41

sleeping on Euston Station.'

'That was only temporary,' Terry said, as though we might have expected him to stay there for the rest of his life. He was behaving quite well with Dad, I have to admit, but showing himself a bit slow on the uptake.

'I've got a chaplain. Tim Rideout. Everyone calls him Timbo.'

'That's not very fair, is it?' Terry seemed concerned at all sorts of injustice, something I rather liked in him.

'Oh, he's proud of his nickname,' Dad reassured Terry. 'He'll expect you to call him Timbo too. Anyway, here's the point. Timbo's dead keen on all sorts of sport. I expect you are too, aren't you, Terry?'

'I haven't had much to do with it. Not for the last three years.'

'I suppose not. But what about boxing? Timbo got a boxing belt when he was up at Keble. Didn't you do a bit of boxing, Terry, before you went away?' my father asked hopefully.

'Not really. A boyfriend of my mum's tried to teach me once. It hurt. That's one of the reasons I left home.' Terry was silent for a minute and then he repeated quietly, 'One of the reasons.'

Dad broke into this moment of clearly unpleasant memory with a cheerful announcement. 'The point is, Timbo has a sizeable flat in the High Street. Church property, of course. He's unmarried and happens to have quite a good-sized spare bedroom.'

'It's a really nice room,' I assured Terry. 'The bathroom's next to it and the Burger King is just down the High Street. You'll like that, won't you?'

42

'And Lucy's going to look round for a job for you,' Dad said. He was full of confidence, even though I had no idea what sort of job it was going to be.

We all of us, including Mum, sat smiling at Terry hopefully at that moment. I'm sure if he'd turned us down and been his usual impossible self I'd have given up being a praeceptor for good.

Terry looked thoughtful and then astounded me by saying, 'Well, thank you very much. I'm extremely grateful.'

You know what about the praeceptor business? I clearly had a talent for it. Something I'd said or done had got through to Terry. It was then that Mum, who came from a nautical family, said, 'The sun's over the yardarm. Who's for a little G&T?'

Terry looked confused so I explained that Mum meant a gin and tonic. He then asked if he could have it without the gin. Mum said, 'I *suppose* you could. But I don't think there'd be very much point in it.' Dad said nothing but handed round the cheesy biscuits in a resigned sort of way.

Later, Dad rang Mr Markby, Terry's probation officer, who approved of our scheme, provided Terry reported to him regularly. 'At times being a bishop comes in useful,' was what my Dad said when he'd put the phone down.

On our way to inspect his new quarters, Terry said, 'Don't you think it's a bit dangerous of your dad?'

'What, finding you somewhere to live?'

'No, keeping his door always open. Don't you remember, that's what he said?'

What I did remember was Terry's long look at Dad's silver loving cup. 'Don't think about it,

Terry,' I said in what I hoped was an impressively warning tone of voice. 'Don't even give it a thought.'

6

'At least we learnt the difference between right and wrong in the Youth Offenders wing.'

Believe it or not, I was sitting with Lucy in the bar of the Intimate Bistro somewhere in Aldershot. I had a Becks beer, my praeceptor had ordered a Pernod with ice and water. The drinks were on her.

'Who taught you that? The chaplain?'

'No! It was the other inmates. They had a code, the inmates did.'

'They taught you morality?'

'They had their morals, yes.'

'What were they exactly?'

'Anything you did wrong to children you got pushed in the scalding shower. No doubt about it.'

'Anything else?'

'You couldn't rob from poor people, like hurt them. There was one big offender there called Jim. He'd set fire to an old tramp asleep on a park bench. He got enough cocoa poured on his head to float a ship.'

'So what *could* you do then?'

'Rob from building societies. Places where they had more money than they knew what to do with. Sort of jobs my Uncle Arthur did but he wasn't all that good at it, half the time.'

'What about breaking into houses by night?'

'Like I said, that was all right. If you stuck to rich people.'

'Lot of Robin Hoods then in the Young Offenders. Stole from the rich. Did they give to the poor?'

'Not often,' I had to admit. 'But your dad, he said it was all right. All of it. I mean, he's a vicar and never heard of hell.'

'You're such an old-fashioned boy.' She seemed to be laughing at me. 'Hell disappeared years ago.'

'I'm not so sure.'

'What a nice old-fashioned boy you are!' she said again.

'That's all right! That's what he said about breaking and entering.'

'I think Robert goes more for understanding than passing judgement.'

'Who's Robert?'

'My dad. Whenever I remember to call him that.'

I looked at her. She had her fair hair parted at the side so it fell across her forehead. Her trousers stopped way before her T-shirt started, leaving her bellybutton open to the world. Her beaten-up old leather jacket was on the seat beside her. She hadn't dressed up at all to visit her mum and dad. Not a bit of it.

Anyway, I've got myself too far ahead, telling you about us sitting at the bar of the Intimate Bistro in Aldershot, waiting for the arrival of its owner, Robin Thirkell, about whom I'll have quite a bit to tell you later.

I suppose I've had low times, like when I stood up in the dock at the Old Bailey and the red-faced judge, with his black cloak and dirty grey wig, who'd been against me from the start, said, 'Keegan, you've clearly grown up to be a habitual criminal. The least sentence I can pass upon you, in the interest of the public, is four years'

46

imprisonment.' But oddly enough, the lowest of all my moments was when I woke up beside a pile of sick in Euston Station. I had no Aunt Dot, no cash and no bed for the night unless I gave into Mr Bloody Markby's hostel. It was then I decided I needed the help of Lucinda (call me Lucy) Purefoy. No question about it.

As you've probably guessed by now, I did find her mum and dad a bit strange. He wore this red shirt with a great big wooden cross hanging over it. But he didn't seem to believe in religion, anyway not as we learnt about it from a teacher at my primary school, who made it pretty obvious that in her view heaven was up there and very pleasant and hell was down below and extremely hot. She also wanted us to be 'born again', which was something I didn't think I could manage, so I didn't pay much attention to her after that. All the same, I didn't think Lucy's dad, the bishop, knew all that much about religion either. And her mother seemed very anxious to get on the sauce, which in her case was gin mixed in with tonic, which was not a drink I could ever stomach at all.

But who am I to criticize after my experience of mothers? In a way I'm sorry for 'call me Lucy' if she hasn't got someone like my Aunt Dot, who was always good to me and kept off the gin. But what did become clear when I was in the palace (so called!) was that they had fixed up somewhere for me to sleep nights and even discussed the situation with the probation officer who delayed my parole.

So I got it clear in my head what I should do. I was going to play along with them as I had with Enhanced Thinking Studies. That way at least I'd get a bed for the night and hopefully a bit of loose change in my pocket and, when that was accomplished, I could walk free of them, just as I'd walked free of prison.

In the end, to help myself towards freedom, I told the dad that I was extremely grateful. When I said that, 'call me Lucy' looked as though Christmas had come and she'd struck lucky with her first offender, who was now well on the way to reform.

All the same, she wasn't so sure of me when we set out to inspect the accommodation at the flat of the person they called Timbo, who seemed to be another sort of chaplain. When I happened to remark that it was a bit unusual of Lucy's dad never to lock a door, she gave me a suspicious look. 'Don't think about it, Terry,' she said. The truth was no decent fence would offer you anything much for a large wooden cross to hang around the neck or even the one small silver cup on the mantelpiece, so I wasn't that interested.

*   *   *

Timbo's flat, however, was absolutely stuffed with silver cups. Sorry. His name was the Rev. Timothy Rideout. It seemed only the bishop called him Timbo and 'call me Lucy' said I was always to say Mr Rideout. Whatever you called him, he was not very tall, with broad shoulders, bright little eyes and hair cropped so short it was almost a number two. He had a sort of soft voice and a funny way of speaking so that the r's came out a bit like w's. All the same, I reckon he must have been strong, because he'd won all these cups for cricket and football and the walls were covered with pictures of the Rev. Timbo holding a bat or a ball in the middle of a team of men who looked much taller than him.

He showed me my room. There was an iron bed and a cross, this time with Jesus on it, hanging beside another photograph of the Rev. Timbo, this time wearing shorts and boxing gloves. I didn't like to say this, but I thought the place looked rather creepy.

'Suit you well, will it?' Timbo looked round at what seemed a bit like a cell without the toilet. 'Better than Wormwood Scrubs anyway.'

'Oh yes,' I told him, my idea being to keep everyone happy till I could plan my escape. 'A whole lot better.'

'Good! Jolly good! Now I'll get the kettle on. I expect you'd like a cup of char?'

Lucy seemed to know that he meant tea. She refused in favour of a cigarette, but I thought I ought to be polite and said I'd have it with milk and sugar. As we sat round in his lounge room with all those teams staring down on us, Timbo looked me straight in the eye and said, 'What's your usual position?'

'I'm afraid my usual position for the last three years has been in one of Her Majesty's prisons.'

'Mr Rideout knows that.' Lucy looked at me as though I'd been particularly slow on the uptake.

'What I meant,' Timbo was smiling as though he could just about tolerate me, 'was your position on the field. Is it in the slips? Silly mid on? Or perhaps you were out at third man?'

'I'm ever so sorry, Mr Rideout. I'm not quite sure what you mean.'

'My dear fellow, have you never played

49

cwicket?'

'Never.'

'Absolutely never?'

'Never at all. We never had a teacher to tell us about it at school.'

'Not wugby? I'm sure you must have played wugby.'

I had to admit that, whatever it was, I hadn't played it.

'Footie then.' Footie seemed to come as the last resort. 'I'm sure you enjoy your footie.'

'Oh yes.' I tried to sound enthusiastic. All I could remember was kicking a ball round the estate with Tiny McGrath and even that usually ended in a fight.

'Sport!' Timbo told us while he poured out mugs of tea. 'That's what'll keep you out of cwime. Cultivate your cwicket. Concentrate on your wugby and you won't go far wrong. Haven't you found that, Lucy, in your life dealing with those who have strayed from the straight and narrow?'

'I really don't know.' Lucy blew out smoke and looked doubtful.

'Take it from me, young lad. Get your head down in a good wugby scwum and you won't want to go thieving any more. It's been an exciting time the past year, hasn't it?'

'Not all that exciting in the Scrubs,' I had to tell him.

'Even there it must have been exciting. Even in Aldershot. I tell you, I had to do a good deal of heavy knee work.'

By now he'd lost me. It was like listening to someone talking a foreign language. What did he mean? Bouncing a ball on his knees to encourage

50

David Beckham? I could only repeat 'knee work' with a big question mark at the end of it.

'On my knees. In the cathedral. Silent prayer, of course. I didn't want to go public. Night and morning at my bedside, I prayed for our success in the European Championships. Heavy, heavy knee work. But Almighty God moves in a mysterious way, as I expect you've found to your cost, Terry.'

I didn't have the answer to that, so I thought it was safer to nod my head and say nothing.

'In his infinite wisdom he decided not to help us when it came to the penalty kicks. Well, there it is.'

'Yes,' said Lucy, stubbing out her fag on one of the Rev.'s saucers. It didn't seem to me that she was enjoying all this talk about God and knee work. 'But we've got no time for playing games. Terry needs a job as well as a bed to sleep in. Thanks, Timbo, we'll be on our way.'

'Yes, of course, Lucinda.' Timbo was on his feet. 'Do send my salutations to the dear bishop. What an inspiration he is to all of us! The photograph on the way out,' he told us as though he was passing on an important secret, 'is Cathedral Clergy and Staff versus the Aldershot Biscuit Factory. What a game that was. Three goals, all in extra time. I'm sure you remember it, Lucinda?'

'No,' 'call me Lucy' told him, 'I don't remember that at all,' which I thought was really rude of her, quite honestly.

*   *   *

So, when I'd planted my toothbrush and toothpaste in Rev. Timbo's bathroom, Lucy took me to the Intimate Bistro. We sat in the small,

51

stuffy bar looking at old French posters showing girls in frilly skirts kicking their legs up, and 'call me Lucy' got her teeth into a strong Pernod and I went no further than a Becks beer. We were waiting, Lucy said, for someone she called Robin ('you'll adore Robin'), who, it seemed, ran the joint but only popped in occasionally.

'My God, what an ass that Timbo is!' Lucy shook her hair out of her eyes and took a big gulp of her white drink.

I told her that I didn't get much help thinking about a life of crime from either the bishop or Timbo. In fact more sense seemed to have been talked about the subject in the Young Offenders wing. So the chat started which kept us going until Robin Thirkell blew in from the street and gave Lucy one of the longest and slushiest French kisses I'd witnessed since before I got four years from Judge Bullingham down the Old Bailey.

7

Although I say it myself, I think this praeceptor business is going rather well. In fact I seem to have quite a talent for it.

I mean, just look at the difference it made to Terry Keegan in only about a week! When I met him coming out of the Scrubs he couldn't have been worse. Rude, sulky, non-cooperative, calling me 'man' deliberately. Stuff like that. I really couldn't find anything good to say about him. And yet only a day later there we were having a drink in Robin's bistro and a really good conversation. He even managed to be reasonably polite to Timbo, who as usual made a bit of an ass of himself talking about his 'wugby'. I remember him taking me to watch that when I was still at school. Quite honestly, I thought it was rather a disgusting game, with grown men pushing their heads up against each other's bottoms. Actually I couldn't see the point of it.

I'm not quite sure if prison works, I'd probably need a bit more convincing, but, as I say, the praeceptor business seems to be working excellently, as witness our conversation about crime and so on in Robin's bistro.

I haven't told you about Robin, have I? I should do, as he's been quite important in my life and will have more than a bit part to play in this story as it unfolds. I mean, I went out with Robin after I'd finished with my old boyfriend Jason and before I met my boyfriend at the time of this story, Tom. I suppose I'd have to admit that Robin Thirkell was the most interesting of the three of them.

He owned not only the Intimate Bistro but also Nifty's, the dress shop in the High Street. He was always looking out for the latest trends and was so cool that one of the local newspapers actually called him 'the Giorgio Armani of Aldershot'. He had a suntan almost all the year round, which I think owed a good deal to Tone Up, the local health and fitness club, but it suited him rather, as did the shades he wore even on grey and cloudy days.

Robin talks in a sort of mocking and dismissive way about most things, but there is a serious side to him. For instance, he makes quite a lot of money, I mean serious money, out of property. Lots of pubs are closing and Robin bought some of them up and turned them into desirable residences for weekenders. He's obviously charmed someone on the local county council, so he doesn't have any problems about getting planning permission, or getting girlfriends if I have to be honest. I've heard some farmers say, if you want foreign workers to pick your fruit or dig your potatoes, you just have to get in touch with Robin and he'll find them for you at a reasonable rate.

Anyway, having fixed a bed for Terry, I had to get him a job and I thought immediately of Robin. I mean, Tom wouldn't be much help. He couldn't find Terry a job in television as he couldn't even get one for himself.

Gwenny in the SCRAP office had explained to us that our 'clients' found it hard to get work because people who might employ them checked up on their criminal records. If they'd been caught thieving, as Terry had far too often, the job offer was off. So, by and large, I thought Robin was the best hope in the world for Terry, who wasn't even an illegal immigrant.

Robin arrived, as usual, late and apparently in a desperate hurry, nicely browned by Tone Up and smelling strongly of Gucci aftershave. He gave me an enormous and long-lasting kiss, which reminded me of old times, and when I emerged from it I introduced him to Terry, who he'd ignored totally up to then.

'Is this your little criminal, Lucy? How tremendously exciting!'

I could see that this particular remark had not gone down at all well with Terry, so I did my best to save the situation. 'He's not especially little and he's not a criminal any longer. So, Robin, it's up to you to give him a job in the Intimate Bistro.'

'Can he wash up?'

'I should think so. You'd better ask him.'

'All right then, Terry whatever your name is, can you wash up? Clear tables? Bring a few dishes in occasionally?'

'Course I can.'

It was obvious that Terry had not yet fallen victim to Robin's undoubted charm. I thought he thawed a bit, however, when Robin said, 'How about £120 a week?'

*   *   *

After that first talk in the Intimate Bistro it wouldn't be an exaggeration to say that I became good friends with Terry. We had more chats in the bar of the bistro and two or three times we drove out into the country in the distinctly clapped-out old Polo I mainly keep at home. He talked to me about his ghastly mum (neither Terry nor I seem to have had much luck in the mum department) and it was clear how much he had loved his Aunt Dot, although his Uncle Arthur obviously suffered from extreme praeceptor deprivation and couldn't help reoffending, which accounted for his continued absence from home when Terry was young. Now he was out of the Scrubs, with a job which, he was glad to say, saved him from Timbo's cricket and wugby chat in the evenings.

Anyway, we were getting on so well and the days were full of spring sunshine and I thought Terry probably hadn't had many picnics in his life, so why shouldn't we have one? I got things together and Terry brought some bits of salami and pâté, together with a bottle of red Rioja which he might or might not have stolen from the bistro. But anyway, I thought, Robin could well afford it and he probably wouldn't have minded. And why would I want to spoil a picnic lecturing Terry again on how to be honest? Instead we drank Rioja out of plastic cups and laughed at something, I can't quite remember what because now, after all that's happened, it seems a long time ago.

When we'd almost finished the Rioja, I asked him how he liked his new job.

'Not bad. It doesn't pay so well as my old one.'

'You mean thieving?' I felt I had to say it, although I still didn't want to lecture him.

'Well, yes. I didn't do no crime for nothing, you know. Not like that mad Russian.'

'Which mad Russian was that?'

'The one who hit the old pawnbroker woman with an axe. Sort of just for the hell of it.'

56

'You mean you've read *Crime and Punishment*?' I knew what I sounded, I sounded patronizing.

'Course I have. Do you think I haven't read books? I've read Charles Dickens.'

'Really? Which one?' I was still sounding patronizing.

'The one where the boy finds the old con in the marshes and gives him a slice of the ham. Something like my Uncle Arthur that old con was.'

'I suppose so,' I said, although I couldn't see the connection.

'*Wuthering Heights*. That was a good one. *Wuthering Heights*.'

I have to say I was surprised at the width of Terry's reading, and realized that there was undoubtedly a good deal more to him than met the eye.

'You surprised I've read books?' He was smiling at me, although probably as aware of my patronizing tones as I was. 'I tell you, you get lots of time for reading in the Scrubs. Probably I've read more books than you have.'

'Probably.' I looked at him. He was still smiling and he looked younger than he had done at any time since I met him at the prison gates. The way he looked, I thought he might be going to make a pass at me, but he didn't.

Instead he stuffed what remained of the food into my basket. But things were definitely better between us. I looked forward to his company and things stayed that way until an evening I'm about to describe and another parting.

* * *

57

'It's all gone extraordinarily well,' I told my boyfriend, Tom, when he came down to stay with me at my parents' place and we were having dinner, just the two of us, in the Intimate Bistro. Tom had told me he'd given up looking for a job in a television company and was spending his time writing a documentary script about the tube called *Underground*, which he was sure any television company would want to do when it was finished. So we were both in a good mood, holding hands and smiling at each other when we'd finished our platefuls of coq au vin and offerings of fresh, locally grown veg.

'It wasn't too easy at first,' I told Tom. 'I felt he resented me. He thought he could do it all on his own, without any support. That was a disaster! He ended up sleeping on Euston Station. But then I brought him down here and got him this job and we've kind of, well, hit it off.'

Tom said, 'I hope you haven't hit it off too far. I mean, you don't fancy him, do you?'

'Of course not, darling. It's a purely platonic relationship.'

Looking back on it, what I said may not have been entirely true, but I didn't want Tom to get into one of his depressed and sulky moods and ruin the evening, so I squeezed his hand.

It was then that Terry emerged from the kitchen wearing a striped apron, to collect our plates, piling them up on his forearm with the dish that had contained the locally grown mixed veg balanced a little insecurely on the top. I was pleased to see that he was learning some of the tricks of a professional waiter.

'Terry,' I said. Well, I couldn't just ignore him,

58

could I? 'This is my friend, Tom Weatherby.'

'Lucy tells me you're getting on so well, Terry,' Tom was concerned enough to say, 'and you're enjoying the Intimate.'

'Am I?' Terry's answer was, I thought, quite rude. 'Well, I can see *you* are,' with which he buzzed off with our dirty plates and the dish, as I say, balanced a bit dangerously on his arm. As he pushed open the door and went down the steps into the kitchen, we heard an almighty crash. Terry had clearly dropped the lot. Our dessert, coffee and the bill were served to us by Hermione, who is Robin's current girlfriend, and I saw no more of Terry that night, nor for a good many nights to come.

It was quite late when we got back to the palace. Robert was still up and working in his study, but Sylvia, my mum, had probably, as usual, staggered up to bed. When we found Dad he gave that sort of warm and deeply understanding look he usually saves for people who've lost a husband or wife, or at least a close relation.

'Lucy,' he said as he poured us each a rather small brandy, 'I'm afraid I have bad news for you.'

'Is it Mum?' I steeled myself to listen to an account of one of Sylvia's regular falls in the bathroom.

'No, darling, it's not Sylvia. It's your pupil. The boy you are looking after. It's about young Terry Keegan.'

'He's not hurt?' I found myself unexpectedly anxious.

'No. Not him. So far as I know he's not hurt at all. The one who was hurt was poor Timbo. He rang me about an hour ago. He was in quite a state about it.'

'About what?'

'Now, Lucy, you mustn't let this shake your faith. We must follow the sinner, you and I, down to the end of his chosen path. And we must not lose our faith. Not ever lose it.'

'Perhaps you could tell me what happened.' I'm really fond of Dad, but I was in no mood to hear one of his Radio 4 'Thoughts for the Day'.

'Well, it seems that your Terry came home at about ten o'clock and assaulted Timbo and went off with one of my chaplain's favourite silver cups. The one he got for the inter-denominational boxing tournament. Your friend Terry just walked away with it.'

'Terry attacked Timbo?' I was still trying not to believe it. 'But he had no violence in his record.'

'Well, he has now,' my dad told me. 'Poor Lucy! It just makes your job that bit more difficult, doesn't it?'

Of course, Robert and Sylvia have no objections to Tom and me sharing a bedroom in the palace. 'Sex is rightly regarded by today's Church as one of God's most generous gifts,' was what my dad always said, although I never got used to the idea of Robert and Sylvia having it off and greatly preferred not to think about such things.

So we said 'goodnight' and made our way upstairs, where I found I wasn't at all in the mood for sex. It was a terribly low moment and I was extremely depressed. All the same, I told Tom, 'I'm not going to give up. I'm not going to let Terry have the satisfaction! It was all working so well. I'm going to get him back on the right track again. It's just a temporary setback. I won't let him go.'

60

'Quite honestly,' Tom said, 'I thought he was bloody rude to us in the restaurant.' Which didn't make me feel any better.

8

I have to say that I found her behaviour disgusting. When I got my job with the Intimate Bistro she welcomed Robin Thirkell by allowing him to put his tongue halfway down her neck, or so it seemed to me. Three weeks later, there she is holding hands with this Tom and staring into his eyes as though he was the only man in the world for her.

Do you know what that sort of behaviour reminded me of? It reminded me of my mother. I just couldn't put up with it.

All right, I showed my feelings. There she was pretending she was always in the right, knowing how to behave and teaching it to what her boyfriend Robin called her 'little criminal', i.e. me—and yet there she is putting herself about to all-comers. As I say, like my mum.

I just couldn't be doing with it any longer. All this happened a good three weeks after I'd started work at the Intimate Bistro. Things hadn't been so bad during that time. I did my work, got my 120 a week and, seeing as I lived rent-free with the Reverend Timbo, it wasn't too bad—all things considered.

There were also a number of laughs to be had in the kitchen. The chef was a big fat Scot called Graham, who came down from Glasgow in search of excitement and landed up in, of all places, Aldershot. He cooked with the help of a good many bottles of the house champagne and it was a wonder to me that Robin didn't seem to notice how much he drank.

He had some jokes too which made the girls laugh in the kitchen, except for Hermione, who was Robin Thirkell's other girlfriend, so he didn't do it in front of her. He might say that the cold cucumber soup needed 'just a soupson [I can't spell it] of urine' and add it in. I've also seen him stick a lump of pastry into his armpit 'just to moisten it a wee bit'. I don't think he'd peed into the chicken with wine sauce that Lucy and her then boyfriend, Tom, had that night. Perhaps that was a pity.

Anyway, I made my view of what was going on pretty clear by the way I picked up their plates. I did it quickly and I didn't make any apologies. I left them to whatever they had in mind as quick as I could, with the result that I had a bit of a crash going down the steps to the kitchen. So, to put it mildly, I wasn't in a very good mood when I went home to the Reverend Timbo's. I'd hardly got up the stairs and into the lounge when an extraordinary thing happened. I felt a bloody great bash to my chin, a vicious sort of upper cut which made my head spin and bloody near unhinged my jaw.

When I opened my eyes after this experience, what should I see but the Reverend, who must have been waiting for me behind the door. All he was wearing was shorts, a T-shirt with a picture of Aldershot Cathedral on it, socks and trainers and boxing gloves that looked about the size of footballs at the ends of his white arms. I could also see another fat pair of boxing gloves on the coffee table, beside a picture book of English country churches.

'Come on, Terry,' Timbo was hopping about

shouting. 'I heard you come in downstairs. You get the gloves on and why don't we go a couple of rounds before bedtime? Blow away the cobwebs. A decent punch-up to get rid of your criminal tendencies. I've helped a lot of lads this way.'

And I'm fucked if he wasn't aiming another upper cut at my criminal's chin.

I've got no violence in my record. A lot of them I got to know in the Scrubs were there for violence of various kinds and I could never see the point of it myself. There was no profit in violence of any kind. But this was an exceptional moment. Number one, I was about to get another stunning knock on my jaw, and, number two, I'd had enough of the Rev. jumping about in front of me. Anyway, the next time I'm up for a sentence of any kind, I'll have to ask for the following to be taken into consideration: a couple of knocks to the side of the Rev.'s head, a temporary grip to his throat, a knee in his groin and a bit of a push which saw him and his boxing gloves falling backwards across the coffee table. I'm not proud of this, but I freely admit that's how it happened.

I collected my money, a couple of new shirts I'd bought, my toothbrush etc. On my way out I also collected just one of the Reverend Timbo's silver cups and put it in my bag, just as a memento really.

'Terry, that's my boxing cup. Where're you going with it?' he called out from the chair, where he was making a rapid recovery.

'Away,' I told him. And I left.

9

So far as I was concerned, it was a council of war.

Was I going to let him get away with it? No, I wasn't! Was I going to go on trying to do a bit of good in the world by turning Terry Keegan away from a life of crime no matter how bleak things looked at the moment? Yes, I was!

So that's why I called a council of war at twelve noon in the sitting room of the palace. The interested parties present were my dad, Robert, in the chair, Robin Thirkell, Tom Weatherby and Sylvia, my mother, who, I must say, didn't have much to contribute. Oh, and me of course, as the person primarily responsible for the irresponsible Terry Keegan.

'Tim's not coming,' Robert told us. 'He said he wanted to give young Terry a boxing lesson for his own good, but that your friend reacted in an unsportsmanlike way. Below the belt, Timbo called it.'

'You mean Tim started the fight?' I asked hopefully.

'Oh yes, but purely as a matter of sport.'

'It was all going so well with Terry,' I felt I still had to defend my client, 'until Timbo hit him.'

'I'm not so sure.' Tom, I know, didn't approve of my doing good in the world so far as Terry was concerned. It was as though he was ridiculously jealous of Terry or something. 'He was bloody rude to us in the restaurant and he broke a lot of plates.'

'Oh, everyone breaks plates to start with,' Robin

said (brownie points for him for being cheerfully tolerant). 'I thought you were doing a marvellous job with that young man, Lucy. In fact I'm going to see if I can't get a load of wrong 'uns and help them by finding them jobs at the farm. Loads of fresh country air might make them go straight!'

'Or not,' said Tom, who doesn't like Robin for reasons, I would say, of jealousy. Again, it's ridiculous, because Robin and I haven't done it for a long time now.

'The first problem we have to face,' I did my best to call the meeting to order, 'is Mr Markby, Terry's probation officer.'

'Yes, of course.' Robert nodded, making it perfectly clear that he had no idea what I was talking about.

'Terry's only out on licence,' I told them. 'He has to report to Alex Markby at regular intervals or he'll be back in the Scrubs. And we wouldn't want that, would we?'

Tom looked as though he would rather welcome this solution, but Robin asked, 'What do you suggest we do, Lucy?'

'I propose we ring up Mr Markby and say . . . well, let's say he's living with Robin on the farm.'

'But wouldn't that be a lie?' Tom pretended to ask an innocent question.

'I was visiting the cottage hospital out at Frimley,' began Robert, about to embark on one of his 'Thoughts for the Day'. 'There was an old chap in there, obviously dying. Lung cancer. And he said to me, "Bishop," he said, "it's bad weather now but I'll be in beautiful weather up there, won't I? Sitting on a cloud I'll be, with all angels and me singing and playing on . . . what do they

66

call them?"

' "Harps?" I suggested. 'Of course, we no longer believe in harps and angels sitting on clouds. I don't know how you could sit on a cloud anyway. You'd just fall through! What I mean is that heaven is a state of mind, a oneness with nature, and death is a passage into the universal mind-set. But not angels with harps.' Here my dad uttered a dismissive little laugh. 'Or sitting on clouds. But what did I say to old Paisley—that's the fellow with the lung cancer—"Of course you'll be sitting on a cloud, Ted, and I look forward to joining you there in due course." All I'm trying to say is that on many occasions what many folk call a lie is in fact an act of mercy.'

'All right,' I told them, 'that's decided then. I'll do an act of mercy tomorrow and tell the probation officer that Terry's gone off to live on Robin's farm. Then we'll really start looking for him.'

*   *   *

'Lucinda Purefoy here. I'm ringing about Terry Keegan. I'm his praeceptor. On behalf of SCRAP.'

'Oh yes.' Mr Markby's voice revealed a complete lack of interest in my call.

'I'm just ringing you to report that Terry's changed his address.'

'I know.' This came into my ear accompanied with a heavy sigh which obviously meant, 'When're you going to stop wasting my time?' 'He has to report regularly to me as he's still on licence, you know. He told me about his change of address.'

I thought this was a bit off as I hadn't been able

to find Terry or tell him where we'd pretend he was living. I thought I'd better say my piece pretty quickly.

'He's staying with a family friend, Robin Thirkell, at God's Acre Manor, near Farnham. Terry's going to work on the farm for Robin. I think it will be good for him to be getting some fresh country air.'

'He isn't.'

'What?'

'He isn't getting any fresh country air.'

'Why do you say that?'

'Because he has a room in a maisonette in Connaught Square belonging to a Mr Leonard McGrath, a financial adviser with no convictions or criminal connections of any sort.'

'Well, neither has Robin Thirkell got any criminal connections.'

'That's as may be. If you'd take my advice, Miss Purefoy, did you say your name was? Yes, Purefoy. I remember you from SCRAP. You'd be far better off leaving this sort of job to professionals. We have long experience of keeping discharged prisoners on the straight and narrow. I understand Keegan's helping Mr McGrath in his financial business, so he's doing rather well. Now, if you'll excuse me, I have a great deal of work to do. He's not my only client, you know.'

Then Mr Markby rang off, having achieved number one slot on my list of people I didn't really like at all.

*   *   *

My efforts to do a bit of good in the world had

clearly been the most pathetic failure—it was the second time Terry had walked out on me and by now I had to wonder if I hadn't taken on a hopeless case and there was no point in trying any more. He'd walked out on me without a word of thanks. He hadn't even sent a thank-you letter to Robert for all the trouble my dad had taken over him, and, quite honestly, he's got an awful lot to do being a bishop and all the worrying he has about Sylvia. I suppose that's something I hadn't fully understood about criminals. They're just not the sort of people who write thank-you letters.

Added to which, all the time I'd wasted on Terry had left me a bit short of money, so I decided to take up the job at the Pitcher and Pitcher Advertising Agency, where my immediate boss was a workaholic woman who'd been put in charge of several important accounts ranging from sanitary towels and breath freshener to garden furniture. Robin had gone off on what he called a business trip to Afghanistan, and Tom, my present boyfriend, had got really stuck into his documentary script about the London Underground (railways and not criminals), so that he mostly didn't want to go out in the evenings, or if he did it was to observe tube stations like Dollis Hill and Neasden, where he could record the underground adventures and unusual experiences of typical travellers. He thought this documentary script was going to land him a writer-director's job in television, although I couldn't see it myself. Of course I didn't say so to Tom. What I'm trying to get across is a picture of my life at that particular moment in time, which I can only, quite honestly, describe as dull and boring, with an emphasis on the dull.

Pitcher and Pitcher's offices are in Oxford Street and in my lunch hours I began to leave the garden furniture account with some gratitude and walk round Connaught Square. It's a big square with tall houses, some of which are divided into flats or separate rooms. You go up the front steps and you are met with a row of bells with various names attached to them. I began to walk round the front doors without any luck until, on my second or third visit, I can't remember which, I found it, a card which read 'Leonard McGrath, BSc. Financial Adviser. Environmentally Friendly Investments. Mortgages and Home Loans Negotiated'. I felt a sort of excitement, I don't know why, as though life might get interesting again, as I rang the bell.

'Who's that?' The voice that emerged from the intercom sounded cautious and slightly alarmed. It wasn't Terry's voice.

'My name's Julie Connaught.' I didn't want to warn Terry if he was up there that I was coming back into his life so, rather unimaginatively, I adopted the name of the square. 'I've come for some advice about taking on a mortgage.'

There was a long pause and then the voice said, not quite so suspiciously, 'You prepared to meet the usual fees for a consultation?'

'I suppose so.'

'Come up then. Top-floor maisonette.' There was a loud buzz and the door clicked open and I started to climb endless stairs. Somewhere near the top a tall, thin man with sharp, enquiring eyes was standing outside an open door. He was wearing a sort of Middle Eastern robe with

70

slippers.

'Miss Connaught?'

'Yes. Are you Mr McGrath?'

'Oh yes indeed. We're quite informal in the office here. As you can see, I'm working from home. Have you brought the paperwork with you?'

'No.' I had to think of an excuse. 'I'd imagined we would just have a preliminary consultation.'

'Well, of course. Come right in.' He gave me a curious sort of twisted smile and led me into a room which contained a good deal of white furniture, a large sofa and a complete absence of office desks or computers.

'We like to keep the atmosphere informal for client consultations, Miss Connaught. This is Diane, my secretary.'

Diane was lounging on the sofa, her feet up on a leather stool. I can only describe her appearance as tacky. When I tell you that she was wearing a ridiculously short denim skirt with chains on it, torn fishnet tights, biker's boots, a tight T-shirt with 'Foxy Woman' written on it in sequins and blue varnish on her fingernails which was seriously chipped, you get what I mean. Business in Environmentally Friendly mortgages couldn't have been brisk because she was reading, or at least turning over the pages of, *Heat* magazine.

Mr McGrath invited me to sink into a white armchair, which I did while considering how to introduce the subject of Terry Keegan. He went on about the fee for a preliminary consultation and how he would take all the worries about my mortgage off my shoulders. Looking round the room, I was surprised to see some quite unexpectedly good pictures and then I noticed on the mantelpiece, beside which Mr McGrath was standing, a familiar-looking tall silver cup.

I stood up when Mr McGrath was still wittering on about mortgages, took the cup off the mantelpiece and read, as I had expected, 'To the Rev. Timothy Rideout, Inter-denominational Boxing Trophy: St Crispin's Theological College, 1984'.

'What are you looking at that for?' Mr McGrath was not best pleased at my interest in the cup, and Diane (did I forget to tell you that she had dyed red hair?) looked up from her magazine with obvious suspicion.

'It's just something I seem to recognize,' I told him. Before I could explain myself any further, the door opened and in came Terry, who saw me holding the cup.

'Oh, Terry,' Mr McGrath introduced me, 'this is Miss Connaught, come after some advice about her mortgage.'

'No, it isn't, Chippy.' This seemed to be Terry's name for Mr McGrath. 'It's Lucy Purefoy, come after me.'

'What the hell do you mean?' Mr McGrath, or Chippy as I'm going to call him from now on, looked entirely confused. Then he turned on me in anger. 'Are you going under a false name then?'

'Well, yes.' I had to admit it. 'Entirely false!'

I thought for a moment that Chippy was going to attack me, push me out of the room and hurl me down the stairs. But Terry calmed him down when he said, 'Back off, Chippy. She's a friend of mine.'

10

'Where are you going?' the Reverend Timbo asked me, and my answer was, 'Away.' By that time I had his silver cup in my luggage in spite of the warning Lucy had given me about silver cups in general. I figured that he deserved to lose one to make up for the pain he had inflicted on my jaw.

It's all very well to say you're going away, but where the away is, that's what matters. When I got on the train to London my future was uncertain. I had a bit of money, but not enough to pay for some decent accommodation. I got out of the train at Waterloo and stood for a while looking at people, all going to places with some sort of definite plan in mind.

I arrived in London just before midnight and I spent out on a room in a small hotel near Waterloo, where the bleary-eyed woman in charge looked as though she wasn't used to singles but specialized in odd couples who couldn't go home to their husbands and wives because they were so desperately in need of a fuck. I found a used condom in the empty fireplace and the bed was home to various insects who stung me during the night. In the morning, not wishing to spend any longer in such a place, I decided to give Chippy a tinkle in the faint hope he might have improved since our last meeting.

'Leonard McGrath, Environmentally Friendly Investments, Diane speaking,' was what I got from a girl with a voice like a rusty gate. 'How can I help you?'

'By cutting all the crap,' I told her, 'and giving me Chippy McGrath.'

'You wish to speak with Mr Leonard McGrath?'

'That's the idea behind me ringing up, yes.'

'May I ask who's calling?'

'Tell him it's Terry Keegan. His old friend.'

'Please hold.' I heard her screech, 'Chippy,' faintly and after a considerable wait my old friend came on the line.

'Terry, you old devil! I thought you were coming to stay at the maisonette.'

'So I was. Until you told me not to.'

'Did I? Did I really do that to you, old friend?'

'You did. And you left me to pay for a bottle of champagne at that lousy club of yours. That cleaned me out of my prison money. I had to sleep on Euston Station.'

'Did you really?' Chippy was laughing his head off. 'You still sleeping there, are you?'

'No, I went to Aldershot.' Chippy found this quite funny too. But then he said, 'Come round. There's still a spare bed for you in the maisonette.'

He gave me the address in Connaught Square and it was there I unpacked my toothbrush, shirts and razor in Chippy's spare room. It was when we were sitting in the white armchairs in his lounge room and Diane brought us two large whiskies that I asked Chippy what all the stuff about Environmentally Friendly Investments was about. Was it a cover?

'Call it that if you like, Terry.' He was still finding my reappearance in his life most amusing. 'It's a good friendly cover anyway. You make mention of the environment and everyone's on your side.'

I waited until Diane went out of the room to make us some sandwiches, as I'd eaten nothing since leaving the Intimate Bistro, and then I asked Chippy if he was doing environmentally friendly crime.

'I suppose you could call it that,' he said, still laughing.

'I didn't want to ask you in front of Diane.'

'Oh, she knows all about me. We needn't have any secrets from her.' I thought at the time that was a dangerous situation but I didn't say so. We were chewing smoked salmon sandwiches when Chippy said, 'We can go back to being partners now, can't we, Terry? It'll be quite like old times.'

'Possibly,' was all I said about that. However, I gave Chippy the Reverend's silver cup and explained that I couldn't pay much rent until I found work to do.

'We'll find you work,' Chippy said. 'Don't worry about that. Where did you get this?' He examined the writing on the cup closely.

'I took it from a reverend guy who tried to break my jaw.'

'You mean you nicked it?'

'Exactly.'

'Well, that's encouraging anyway.' Chippy was still looking critically at the article in question. 'You wouldn't get much for it even melted down.'

'I know. I thought you might like to have it. Just as an ornament.'

Chippy stood up and put it on his mantelpiece. 'We'll be partners,' he repeated. 'Just like old times.'

Chippy's spare bedroom was a good deal brighter and warmer than the one I'd had at

Timbo's and for the first time in several years I sank into a really comfortable bed. I also felt at home there, which I'd never felt at Aldershot.

*   *   *

It was like, when I got that upper cut, something snapped inside of me. It was as if I couldn't take it any longer, all these people trying to reform me as though I had some sort of nasty disease which they couldn't quite understand.

It was also that I felt sick of having to be so grateful for everything, from a job in that Robin's bistro where the pay was not all that marvellous, quite honestly, to being socked on the jaw for my own good.

It was also that they seemed sort of excited by the idea of me being an interesting specimen, a real live criminal. 'Is this your little criminal?' was what Robin had said to Lucy, and, 'How tremendously exciting.' So I began to think I was just there as an entertainment which they would get used to and then get bored with the whole business.

So by the time I rang Chippy I'd decided to break with the past, at least as far as Aldershot was concerned. I got Chippy to ring Mr Markby, my probation officer, to tell him that I'd got first-class accommodation with Leonard McGrath of Environmentally Friendly Investments, and a good prospect of getting a job with him eventually.

While I had been away, Chippy had formed an extremely efficient organization. Bent burglar-alarm salesmen gave him news of particularly well-stocked houses. Bent insurers told him where the best pictures and the finest collections of silver could be found. His personal fence had a house in Brighton where art treasures could be turned into ready money, and he even found a bent art expert to tell him which pictures were valuable, but not so famous that you could never get rid of them. Chippy and his associates selected houses from Richmond to Golders Green and Hampstead Garden Suburb.

From time to time, Chippy was even more ambitious. He'd enlarge the team to include a peterman to blow safes. We'd do warehouse breaking and one time we got away with a whole safe full of expensive watches, which sold well from the house in Brighton. The point was that Chippy was in a pretty prosperous line of business and, as luck would have it, I was able to share a bit in his prosperity.

Working with Mr Leonard McGrath of Environmentally Friendly Investments in a number of posh houses to the north of Oxford Street, I earned quite a bit of cash, which enabled me to order drinks, being well able to pay for them, in the Beau Brummell Club, which I no longer considered lousy but an excellent place to meet up with the better quality of blaggers, reliable sources of information, as well as some quite well-known footballers and personalities on television. I went with Chippy at first, but as I gained confidence I started to go on my own and had some quite interesting conversations there.

I suppose it all started again when we got news about a house in Dorset Square which was shared, the information was, by a couple of blokes, one older and the other considerably younger. We got the information from the firm they used for a bit of cleaning. So I was in there one night, sorting out the silver and a few small pictures the insurance people had told us might be worth lifting off the walls, when I suddenly saw it, a photograph pinned to a sort of noticeboard in what I took to be the older chap's study. I'd shone a torch on it during my search of the place and there it was. A group of girls around a grey-haired man in a crumpled suit in front of a door marked 'SCRAP Central Office'. And I saw her among the girls present, smiling out shyly at the camera: Lucinda 'call me Lucy' Purefoy, who had tried to stop me from doing exactly what I was doing when I saw her photograph.

I can't say how I felt. I'd decided to go back to the life I knew and that was it. All the same I felt, well, I won't say it was guilt, but I had to admit Lucy had done her best to help me and we'd also had some good conversations, not like those I got in the Beau Brummell Club but good conversations all the same. And I'd gone off without a single goodbye, which, looking back on it, seemed a bit of a mean way of going on. On the other hand, there was nothing much I could do about it now, so I dismissed her from my mind.

But she kept coming back. I could see her as she was when we chatted in the bistro, fair hair falling across her forehead, her bellybutton out on view, and that look she gave as though she was genuinely worried about me. Of course, I didn't miss her worry, but in some weird sort of way I was beginning to miss her. Perhaps it was because she was so different from Chippy's Diane or the brass you got to meet round the Brummell that I missed

Lucy, but if we ever met again I was certain she would give me up as a hopeless case, certainly not worth any further trouble, so I told myself to stop thinking about her.

As this is to be a story about me and Lucy, I must go on to about three months after I left Aldershot, which would make it June, the start of a grey, wet summer. It seemed that Aldershot and all that happened there was just a distant memory when I walked into Chippy's lounge room and, for God's sake, there she was, looking just as I remembered her, holding the Reverend Timbo's silver cup in her hands and admitting that she had gained access to Chippy's maisonette by the use of an assumed name. I could see that this particular conduct, which I found a bit hard to understand, had irritated Chippy and I told him to calm down because she was a friend of mine, at which I thought Lucy looked surprised and grateful.

Chippy, on the other hand, was not so easily cheered up. 'We don't like people,' he told her, 'who come here pretending to be someone else.'

'I thought,' this was her explanation, 'Terry wouldn't want me to come up if I gave my real name.'

'Why wouldn't Terry want you to come up?' Chippy was always suspicious and probably rightly so. 'There is nothing here in Environmentally Friendly Investments for us to be ashamed of.'

'I'm sure there isn't, Mr McGrath.' She was still smiling, but respectful. 'I'm absolutely sure of it.'

'You come to get Reverend Tim's cup back, have you?' was what I asked her.

'Not necessarily.' And much to my surprise, she put the silver pot in question back on the mantelpiece. 'I came here to find you. I thought we might have a drink together some time. And a bit of a chat. You know, like we did when you were working at the Intimate Bistro.'

She certainly knew the right thing to say because, as I say, that was the chat I remembered. But she wasn't pushy about it, not at all pushy.

'Ring me if you feel like it. I'm working for Pitcher and Pitcher in Oxford Street. Ring me any time.'

She gave me a card, which I put away carefully, and then she left us. When she had gone, Chippy looked unhappy and said, 'What the hell is she? Working for the Serious Crime Squad at Paddington nick, is she? Come here to find things out?'

'She's not working for any nick, you can be sure of that.'

'All right then. But she's your responsibility, Terry. I'll hold you responsible for her and anything she might do uncalled for. I want you to be aware of that.'

I told him I was well aware.

11

Of course I never expected to hear from him again.

So I worked away at Pitcher's and they gave me an account (Tell-All Beachwear) of my very own and Tom stayed with me in my one-bedroom flat in Notting Hill and nothing enormously exciting was happening at all.

Oh, I should record the fact that Mr Orlando Wathen from SCRAP rang me and asked me if I was still seeing my client Keegan. For some reason I told him that I hadn't seen Terry for a while and that I'd rather lost touch with him.

'Typical,' Orlando said. 'Entirely typical. You can't do anything for some of these little bastards. Hopeless cases, entirely hopeless!'

'Do you really think so?'

'I know so. Let me tell you. Peter and I were away at our place in the Dordogne and they got into Dorset Square. All the silver has gone and some pretty valuable pictures. I'm sorry, Lucy, the only place for some of these little menaces is back in the prisons where we found them.'

'You never discovered who did it?'

'Of course not! And the police can't be bothered to find out. Longer sentences. That's the only answer.'

'Is that SCRAP policy from now on?' I was more than a little surprised and wondered if Gwenny now supported that view.

'SCRAP? Oh, I'm leaving SCRAP. I'm doing voluntary work at the Home Office. Advising on the parole system.'

'You think we should have more of it?'

'No. Far, far less. Keep in touch. The Home Secretary wants more information about failures in the praeceptor system.'

After that I didn't think I'd be hearing much more from SCRAP and then, one morning at work, the switchboard girl told me that someone called Terry Keegan was on the phone, so I said, 'Put him through,' and there he was, sounding more calm and self-confident than I ever remembered.

'Where've you been hiding, Lucy?' he said, as though it was my fault. 'What about meeting up for a drink or something?'

'Of course, I'd like that. Where exactly?'

'How about my club?'

'What's your club then,' I asked. 'The Athenaeum?'

I had a momentary absurd vision of Terry in the bar of the Athenaeum in Pall Mall (Robert of course belongs to it), holding forth to an audience of senior civil servants, judges and professors of history on life in the Scrubs.

'It's the Beau Brummell in Harrowby Street. I think you'll find I'm pretty well known there.'

'I'm sure you are.'

'Would you be free Thursday, shall we say round six o'clock?'

'Why ever not?'

Terry's club turned out to be a far cry from the Athenaeum. There were two large and burly men wearing top hats at the entrance who I took to be bouncers. They gave me the sort of amused and condescending look of those who knew single women only entered the Beau Brummell for one reason and they might expect to get a cut of anything she earned there. The girl at the desk said that Mr Keegan was waiting for me in the club room and I went up in the lift to find him.

Of course the Brummell bore very little resemblance to what I remember of the Athenaeum when Robert took me there. Pools of light lit up the tables, where girls wearing bow ties and very little else were dealing out cards or spinning roulette wheels. There were hardly lit areas where large men and shadowy women were sitting talking. The whole place smelt of perfume and air freshener with a distinct undercurrent of the burning old-carpet odour of pot. Under the tactfully dimmer lights of the bar, I saw Terry sitting beside an ice bucket and a bottle of champagne.

He was wearing a dark suit and, extraordinarily enough, a tie, his hair was neatly brushed and he gave off an expensive smell of aftershave. If I didn't know, I'd have put him down as some high-flying broker from the City.

'Hello there,' he said. 'Can I offer you a glass of bubbles?'

I said I didn't see why not and then there was a silence, as though neither of us was quite prepared to explain the strange situation in which we now found ourselves. Then he said, 'I brought you this.' He fished up a plastic bag from the floor beside his bar stool. 'He can have it back,' he said.

It, of course, was Timbo's boxing cup.

'Are you sure?' I had made a point of leaving it with him as a recompense for Tim's ridiculous attack.

'Of course I'm sure. Anyway, you couldn't get much for it, not from anyone dealing in such things.'

'And do you know anyone dealing in such things?'

'Perhaps.' He seemed determined not to give too much away. 'From the old days, of course.'

'So, thank you for giving this back.' I put Tim's cup beside my stool. I'd scored a bit of a praeceptor's success, although Orlando Wathen might not be pleased with me.

'Have you got a job now, Terry?'

'Oh yes. I've got a job.'

'What is it exactly?'

'Helping Chippy out with his business.'

'You mean the Environmentally Friendly Investment business?'

'That's the one.'

'It must be doing pretty well.'

'It's doing all right. Yes.'

Before I could ask any more about Chippy's to me rather mysterious investment business, Terry, whom I saw looking towards the roulette table, gave a great shout of 'Sandy!' At which a pink-cheeked plump little man, wearing a deafening Hawaiian patterned shirt and lightweight suit, got up and crossed towards us to greet Terry with a quick embrace.

'This is Sandy, a friend of my Uncle Arthur's.' Terry introduced us in a way I found even more encouraging. 'This is Lucy, a friend of mine.'

'Good to meet you, Lucy.' Sandy took my hand and pumped it energetically. 'Your Uncle Arthur, Terry,' he said when he'd finished with my hand, 'dreadful bad luck that was, the job he got put away for.'

'I was away myself,' Terry explained. 'I don't really know what happened.'

Sandy looked at me doubtfully for a moment and then said, 'Can we talk freely?'

'Quite freely,' Terry assured him. 'Lucy's used to it. Her father's a bishop.' I suppose this was meant to be a joke. He was obviously in a good mood.

What Sandy wanted to say was that Uncle Arthur was doing ten years for his part in an armed robbery.

'The Bright Penny Friendly Society office in Peckham. They kept a lot of cash there,' Sandy was explaining to me as though to a child. 'Of course, he never ought to have got caught. It was all Jim Nichols's fault. A tragedy really, but we had to laugh.

'They're in the getaway car, with Big Jim Nichols driving, and the rozzers that got called after the party was over chasing them. They're going fast, with your Uncle Arthur in it, when the freestanding phone in the car rings and this male voice asks, "Hello, is Jim Nichols there?" So Jim answers, "Yes," and the voice goes on, "This is Chris Tarrant from *Who Wants to Be a Millionaire?*" You know what the game *Millionaire* is, don't you?' The man in the Hawaiian shirt looked at me as though I might not know anything about contemporary life.

'Yes,' I said, 'I do know about *Millionaire.*'

'All right then. So Chris Tarrant goes on, "We've got your friend Harry Stoker here in the studio and he's doing rather well. In fact he's up to £32,000, but he's stuck on one question so he's chosen you as his friend."

'"OK," Big Jim Nichols says, this being the most bloody foolish thing he's ever done, "put him on."'

For any of you—and I can't imagine that there *are* any of you—who don't know, *Who Wants to Be a Millionaire?* is a programme on television in which Chris Tarrant is the quizmaster and competitors, who may win large sums of money, are allowed to phone a friend to help them with one of the general knowledge questions.

'"The next voice you hear will be Harry's and he has one question with four possible answers." Apparently Jim had foolishly agreed to be a friend that evening.

'"You ready, Jim?"

'"Yes, mate," Jim says, already slowing down slightly.

'Harry said, "The question is, which king died of a surfeit of lampreys? Was it a) King John, b) King Charles I, c) King Harold or d) King Henry I?"

'"King Charles I?" Big Jim wondered out loud, and it seems your Uncle Arthur chipped in with, "No. It couldn't be him. He died of having his head chopped off." And then they were all arguing about who died of lampreys and what lampreys were anyway, and Jim slowed down so much that the rozzers got them, each and every one of them. Funny, isn't it? I heard the story from a bloke who was with your Uncle Arthur in Parkhurst. Most unfortunate, but I had to laugh.'

I had to laugh too, but Terry looked serious. 'I never heard that,' he said. 'I never heard about my Aunt Dot either.'

'No. She was a good woman was your Aunt Dot. Helped me out a few times, I can tell you. There's

Rosanne waving at me. I've got to go back to her.' He was looking towards a woman in a green top who was signalling to him from the roulette table.

'I told Rosanne she brought me luck sitting beside me,' Sandy was still laughing at the misfortunes of life, 'and when I lose, like I have been doing, I tell her that I'd have lost a lot more if she hadn't been there.' So he went off, apparently cheerfully.

'I never knew all that about Uncle Arthur,' Terry repeated, without smiling, when we were left alone together. His mood seemed to have deteriorated a bit.

'You know,' I said to him, 'all that Environmentally Friendly Investments stuff is a load of nonsense, isn't it?'

'What do you mean?' He began to look angry and defensive.

'I mean that whatever's bought you a new suit and a tie and a bottle of bubbles in this extraordinary club wasn't investments that were at all friendly to the environment.'

There was a bit of silence after that. He was frowning as he said, 'You still trying to reform me, are you?'

If I said yes I knew we'd lose contact altogether, so what I said was, 'Certainly not! I gave you up months ago as a completely hopeless case.'

'A hopeless case, am I?'

'Absolutely.'

'So you gave up on me?'

'What else could I do?'

'Yeah,' he said thoughtfully. 'What else could you do? You lot will never begin to understand.'

'Which lot?'

'The lot that tries to reform people. And that.'

'You mean we don't understand why you need smart suits and maisonettes, fast cars and all that sort of thing?'

'I haven't even got a car.'

'Haven't you? Poor Terry!' I pretended to sound terribly sorry for him.

'I could fix myself up with one of course. In time of need.'

'Oh good.'

'None of you understands the real reason.'

'And what is the real reason, Terry?'

By now Terry had drunk most of the champagne. I'd had a glass, which wasn't really as good as the house stuff at the Close-Up. But whether or not the drink, such as it was, had loosened his tongue, I don't know, but what Terry said then had a profound effect on me and, indeed, on the rest of this story.

'It's the excitement. That's what you lot don't understand.'

'What do you mean, the excitement?'

'People do all sorts of dangerous things, don't they? They climb up bloody great precipices. They set out to walk to the North Pole, or drop out of aeroplanes or try to cross the Atlantic in a canoe or something equally daft. What do they do it for? The excitement. I tell you honestly, Lucy, all that's nothing compared to the excitement of a decent bit of crime.'

'You mean pinching things?' It was the longest speech he'd ever made to me.

'All right then. Pinching things. Even taking Rev. Timbo's bloody boxing cup gave me a little bit of a thrill when I nicked it.'

'Now you're giving it back.'

'Of course.' Terry sighed as though I was extremely slow on the uptake. 'It was taking it that was worthwhile. The pot's hardly worth trying to flog down the pub on a Saturday night.'

'You mean you've found other crimes much more exciting?'

'Tell you a story,' Terry said. 'I remember what my old Uncle Arthur told me about his friend Springy Malone, so called because he could hop across roofs and so forth. Well, Springy did serious crime until he got reformed and took up religion. But he told Arthur how disappointing it was when he went to the bank to draw out a pile of money for his house repairs or his wife support or something. He stood watching the cashier count it out and he thought, in the good old days I'd have pulled out a shooter and taken the lot off you. How dull life has become! Can you understand that?'

'I might try to.'

'Forget all the mountain climbing and falling out of aeroplanes and all that. Being in someone else's house at night. Getting the silver out of the drawers and the money out of the safe and the pictures off the walls and wondering all the time if they're going to wake up and you'll be caught and put away for another few years or so. I tell you, Lucy, there's nothing so exciting. People can't get cured of it.'

'You mean you can't.'

'You still don't understand it,' he said, not angrily, but smiling. Then he picked up his cuff to display a classy sort of watch which I hadn't seen before. 'I've got to go,' he said, 'I've got an appointment.'

'With Environmentally Friendly Investments?'

'Something like that, yes.' It was not really that he seemed, at that moment, better-looking, more in control, than he ever had before. It was like, quite honestly, that he was going off into a world in which there was no place for me at all.

'But like I said,' he went on, 'you lot will never understand it. You may have given up trying to reform me. But you'll never understand why we want to do it. Got to go now.' And then he smiled unexpectedly. 'We might do this again. Some time soon.'

'Yes,' I said, 'some time soon.'

He left me then. I had a moment's fear that he might have landed me with the bill, but no, it had all been paid for.

On my way out I passed Sandy and saw a great pile of his chips being raked away on the roulette table. In spite of his bad luck, he waved a cheerful goodbye. I waved back, happy to feel at that moment a small part of Terry's world. The truly worrying thing, I realized, was that I had done what no decent praeceptor should ever do—fallen in love with the client.

12

'I just rang to see how you were getting on with your client. It's young Terry Keegan, isn't it?'

'Yes, it is. I think we've reached a pretty good understanding.'

'He's kept out of trouble?'

'So far, yes. I don't think he's in any trouble at all.'

Gwenny had called me at Pitcher's and, for the moment, I seemed able to give satisfactory answers to all her questions. Then she said, 'We're having a bit of trouble here at SCRAP.'

'Oh, I'm sorry to hear that.'

'Orlando Wathen resigned. He suddenly announced that the main cause of crime was the soft and soppy liberal view we took of it in the sixties.'

'Is that true?'

'I don't know. I can't begin to think about it now. Anyway, Orlando wrote to the *Daily Telegraph* calling for life sentences for a second conviction for house-breaking.'

'Did that have something to do with the fact that his house was broken into?'

'I think it may have done. Anyway, we couldn't have the head of SCRAP saying things like that, so he resigned and we're looking for a replacement. That's why I rang you actually.'

'Why?'

'Alex Markby said there's a wonderful chap called Leonard McGrath. Apparently he's done good things for the environment. But he also said

91

that he'd found a job for your client, Terry Keegan, and helped him go straight since he came out of the Scrubs. Do you know anything about him?'

'Oh yes. I know quite a lot about Leonard McGrath.'

'Alex thinks he has great organizing ability. Is that right?'

'I should say his organizing ability is terrific.'

'That's good to know. You haven't met him, have you?'

'Oh yes. I've met him.'

'Do you think he'd be interested in helping young criminals? Will you have a word with him?'

'Yes, I will. And I think he might be very interested.' I had to put the phone down before I started to giggle.

Anyway, I had more important things to do than talk to Gwenny when I felt, quite honestly, more than a little guilty having broken the first rule of a praeceptor. I had to go down to my parents in Aldershot because it was the weekend and I meant to restore at least one of Terry's ill-gotten gains to its rightful owner.

*　　　*　　　*

'Timbo will be delighted,' Robert said when I got down to Aldershot.

'Delighted to get his pot back?'

'Delighted that young Terry repented. There is more joy in heaven over one sinner that repents than over ninety and nine just persons who need no repentance.'

'I'm not so sure about his repenting. Apparently

92

he couldn't get much for the cup, even down the pub on a Saturday night.' I was trying to bring Robert down to the harsh reality of the situation, but he was off on another 'Thought for the Day'.

'Rather odd that, you may think. I mean, it seems, on the face of it, a bit unfair on the ninety and nine just persons who don't get God's attention at all. What He really likes are the sinners. Are we to understand that He created them in order that He might have the pleasure of seeing them repent? How many of us are troubled, deeply troubled, by that thought?'

'Not many of us,' would have been my answer. 'In fact hardly anyone at all.' But I didn't want to spoil what Robert told me would be the theme of his Sunday sermon in the cathedral. Then he changed the subject.

'So you have done a splendid job with young Terry, Lucy. And I'm sure both God and my chaplain are extremely grateful.'

I could have woken Robert up to the reality of life as led by members of the Beau Brummell Club, but this would have been unnecessarily cruel. 'And tonight we're invited for drinks with the dear Smith-Aldeneys,' my dad told me. 'You remember them, don't you, Lucy?'

'Of course. I used to go to pony club with Persephone.'

'They're good people. She does a lot for charity and he's chair of the Save the Cathedral Committee. They do excellent work, but I'm afraid they're part of the ninety and nine just persons who bore God. They bore me too, if I have to be entirely honest about it.'

'But we're going to drinks with them?'

'In this life, Lucy, we must take the rough with the smooth,' my dad told me. 'We can only pray for something more entertaining in the life to come.'

There was nothing really wrong with the Smith-Aldeneys. In fact they did everything right. They lived in just the right size of converted farmhouse to the south, that is to say the better, side of Aldershot. They had just the right amount of land, a large garden and a paddock for the ponies. They had just the right amount of money since Christopher Smith-Aldeney worked for a City bank, and the right number of children. Persephone, who was my age and just returned from backpacking in Cambodia, an experience which seemed to have changed her not at all, and a younger son, Billy, who was reading economics at Cardiff. Their mother, Olive Smith-Aldeney, controlled the whole family with determined charm. You could be quite sure at a party of the Smith-Aldeneys that nothing embarrassing or outrageous would occur and probably nothing very interesting either.

Then the usual harmless calm of drinks with the Smith-Aldeneys was broken, of course, by Robin, who said, 'There's a sort of glow about you, Lucy. Have you been fucking that little criminal of yours?'

'Of course not! Don't be ridiculous!' I told him. Fortunately Persephone came up to us and wanted to discuss three-day eventing and the time when we were all at pony camp together, and Robin drifted away before he could come out with any more stupid and unfounded accusations.

And then of course Christopher Smith-Aldeney came up and asked if I'd like to see his collection of ancient coins and 'my new acquisition'. Long ago, when I was about fourteen, I'd shown a sort of polite interest when Christopher showed me his coins and he had been sure that I was a budding numismatist, if that's the right word. So I never visited Fallowfield, the Smith-Aldeneys' home, without Christopher opening his glass cases and taking me on a brisk tour through the ducats and Louis d'ors, the crowns and the florins, the Arab coins stamped with Christ by the crusaders, the first pounds of the British Raj in India and the ancient coinage of Mesopotamia centuries before it had been turned into Iraq, as Christopher was never tired of telling me. But now there was something entirely new—a Roman coin with the head of the Emperor Claudius discovered by a metal detector in a field near St Albans. He told me what he'd paid for it and said it had given an entire lift to his collection.

'Don't you think it's beautiful, Lucy?' Christopher said, and although it seemed a rather ordinary bit of bronze to me, I agreed that it brought the whole history of the Roman Empire back to the drinks party in Fallowfield. With that he gave me the squeeze which brought him into close contact with my tits and the sort of distinctly damp kiss I used to get when I came back to the farmhouse after gymkhanas and pony club events with Persephone.

However, just as Christopher was uttering the corniest of lines and giving me the usual not entirely welcome squeeze, Mrs Smith-Aldeney came up considerably worried, not about her husband's squeezing but about the conduct of my mother. 'Sylvia says she didn't come out to drink

95

sherry in glasses the size of eggcups and could she have a G&T. I told her I'd ask you to find something or other.' At which her husband put his Claudius coin down on the table beside his glass cases and went buzzing off in search of a bottle of gin.

'I'm terribly sorry,' I told Olive after Christopher had gone.

'What've you got to be sorry about, Lucinda?' Olive wasn't in the best of tempers.

'My mum,' I told her.

'Oh, don't you worry.' Olive became most sympathetic. 'We've got used to her.'

I left the party as Christopher was administering a large gin to my mother, and I drove myself straight back to London as I had to be up early for a breakfast meeting with the Tell-All Beachwear account. I'd hardly started when my mobile rang its little tune ('Toreador') and Christopher was sounding desperate.

'Lucy!' he said. 'I've lost the Claudius coin.'

'You can't have done.'

'I thought I put it back in the case. But when I'd given your mother her drink and talked to a few people and the party was nearly over I looked and it wasn't there.'

'How extraordinary!'

'You didn't see what I did with it?'

'I'm afraid not. But I'm sure it will turn up somewhere.'

'I've searched every corner of the room.'

'And you couldn't find it?'

'Nothing so far. It's a complete mystery.'

'Yes,' I said. 'I suppose it is.'

13

'Let me see now. You're still working with Environmentally Friendly Investments?'

'Oh yes, I am.' I told Mr Markby, my probation officer, nothing but the truth.

'Good! I'm glad to hear it. There's nothing more vitally important in our world today than global warming.'

'Oh, I agree. It's in my thoughts twenty-four hours a day.'

This was a bit of a lie, because global warming scarcely ever crosses my mind. But Mr Markby looked pleased and said, 'Good, very good!' and ticked another box on his form.

'I sometimes wonder how you managed to land a job with Mr McGrath. Have you had any training in business studies?'

'Not much,' I had to admit. 'I think he took me on as a favour.'

'Leonard McGrath wanted to help you go straight!' Mr Markby seemed deeply impressed. 'How long have you known him?'

'I was at school with his young brother.'

'At school with Leonard McGrath's brother?' Mr Markby was being a bit of an echo.

'Yes, I was.'

'Well, look what he's made of his life. Runs his own important business. That should've been an example to you.'

'Well yes. It has been in a way.'

'Good. Excellent.' Mr Markby seemed easy to please that day. 'They're looking for a new man to

97

head up SCRAP. I put Leonard McGrath's name forward. I hope he won't mind.'

'I'm sure he'll be pleased.' Of course I could see the funny side of it. Then my probation officer leaned back in his chair and said, 'By the way, are you seeing any more of your so-called praeceptor, that Miss Purefoy?'

'Not much.' I lied again. I didn't think he needed to know about my friends.

'Good. I'm glad of that. Those girls rush in where we probation officers are careful where we tread. She was obviously misinformed as to your place of residence. She said you were staying on some farm somewhere. You weren't, were you?'

'Never.'

'I thought not. Well, my advice to you is to give that Miss Purefoy a wide berth.'

'All right then.'

'So long as you hold down your job with Mr Leonard McGrath . . .'

'That's just what I mean to do.'

'And report to me regularly, I'm quite happy.'

I'd never really forgiven Mr Markby for delaying my parole, although he seemed a good deal more friendly since I moved in with Chippy. There was one piece of his advice, however, that I was determined not to take, and that was the bit about giving Lucy 'a wide berth', which I suppose meant I mustn't see her again.

Well, the hell with that, Mr Markby. It was a bit surprising at the time, but it seemed that I wanted to see Lucy more than ever I had before. I suppose life's like that, isn't it? When she was busy trying to reform me I wanted to get as far away from her as possible. But when she said she'd given me up as a bad job I felt I couldn't get enough of her. It wasn't just the way she looked, I swear to you it wasn't. Of course she looked the sort of girl you're proud to have sitting next to you at the bar of the Beau Brummell. I'd found out you could have a good conversation with her, and good conversations weren't easy to come by around the maisonette.

So I was seriously thinking of giving Lucy a bell again, but before I got round to doing that she rang me at the maisonette and sounded, I thought, a bit less confident and sure of herself than usual.

'I wonder if you'd like to go out with me some time. Have dinner together or something?' You see what I mean? That wasn't the usual Lucy, who knew exactly what she wanted. It also reminded me of the different sort of worlds we came from. When I was a kid, 'dinner' was something you only got on Sundays if you were lucky. What you had in the evening was your 'tea'. Now I'd drifted up in the world of dinner eaters, like Chippy McGrath and Lucy Purefoy.

'No,' I said. 'I'll take you out.' Let her pay a bill, I thought, and she'll be back feeling she's in control and trying to reform me. 'Shall we say Thursday?' That wasn't too soon, although I wasn't doing anything in particular on the other nights of that week.

'I'd love to see you on Thursday.' She seemed to be genuinely pleased.

'All right, I'll ring you. Time and place. I'll pick a good one.'

The truth was that I had no idea where to pick. I had to consult a well-known member of the smart set—Mr Leonard McGrath.

'The in place now is definitely La Maison Jean

Pierre,' Chippy told me. 'Jean Pierre is a personal friend. Your girlfriend's going to love it.'

'All right then, but she's not my girlfriend.'

'Only trouble is . . . you won't get a table in less than six months' time.'

'We can't go there then.'

'Unless we ask for it in my name. Lift the phone, would you, Diane? When do you want to go?'

'Say . . . Thursday?'

'Oh, it's Leonard McGrath's office here,' Diane told the 'in place'. 'Mr McGrath would like a table for two on Thursday. Yes, dinner. Shall we say eight o'clock? Cool.' She put down the phone. 'They're looking forward to seeing us.'

'But they'll be seeing *me*.'

'Just say I came down with a heavy cold,' Chippy told me, 'so I sent you to take my place as you run my accounts department and it's your birthday.'

I rang Lucy in her office as I couldn't get an answer from her flat. 'I'll pick you up at your place in a taxi,' I told her.

'No, no, don't do that. I'll meet you at the restaurant. Where are we going?'

'La Maison Jean Pierre.'

'You're not serious?'

'I may not be, but I'm still taking you to La Maison Jean Pierre. Apparently it's the in place nowadays.'

'Who told you that? Leonard McGrath at Environmentally Friendly Investments?'

'Perhaps.'

'All right then, I'll meet you there.' She was laughing. I couldn't tell why us going to this place to eat had amused her so much.

*　　　*　　　*

The restaurant, when we got into it, wasn't all that funny either. It was in a room with white walls and steel furniture, like the sort of place you expect to see on a hospital wing. There were a few pictures on the walls, but they didn't seem to be pictures of anything, just plain colours. They were the sort of thing I'd have left on the walls of any house I'd broken into. It's true the place was very full and busy and it was quite a while before some sort of top waiter arrived and told us what to order. 'Tonight, Jean Pierre recommends,' he said, and made it clear that it was what we'd choose unless we were a couple of idiots who'd never seen the inside of a five-star restaurant before. He had tight lips and was just as determined to control my choices as Mr Markby, my probation officer.

I can't remember much about the food we ate except it was a big let-down and, on the whole, pretty disgusting. The idea of a good feed never seemed to have entered the mind of Jean Pierre or his kitchen staff. The starter was something to do with marinated seaweed, which wasn't anything I'd have to eat again. The fish didn't look much like any fish I'd ever met before and had a taste of meat about it, and a salad of plums and raspberries, with not a chip in sight. On the whole I think we did better, food-wise, in the Burger King in Notting Hill. Not much of that's worth remembering, but what I'll never ever forget is what happened when all this rubbish had been cleared away and all we had was two cups of coffee on the table. All we had, that is, until Lucy produced—well, I'll have to tell you what she

101

produced and perhaps it'll surprise you as much as it surprised me.

She'd been sort of excited during the meal with lots of 'Mmmmm, this is delicious!' which I think she did more out of politeness to me than because she genuinely enjoyed what we were eating. And then, when we got to the coffee part, she was, as I've said, excited.

She opened her handbag and put something down on the tablecloth.

'I got this for you,' she said.

What she'd got was a dirty old coin that might have been shiny years and years ago but was now a sort of dull green colour—I picked it up and I could just make out a bald head and some letters I could hardly read.

'That's very kind,' I said. I didn't want to seem ungrateful. 'Did you buy this for me?'

'No,' she said, and by now she was almost laughing. 'I stole it for you.'

'You did *what*?' I was so surprised that I asked her while the waiter was hovering.

She was a bit more cautious, she only said, 'I told you what I did.'

'But *why*?' I asked her as the waiter moved away. It seemed like, well, like the whole world had turned upside down.

'I suppose because I wanted to understand you properly.'

'Understand me? Am I so peculiar or something?'

'It was what you said about the excitement. You said it was the extraordinary excitement that made you do it.'

'That's part of it, of course.'

'Part of it? It seemed to me the way you said it, it was the whole of it.'

'And earning a living, of course.'

'I suppose there is that,' she seemed a bit disappointed, 'but you said it was the excitement you'd miss.'

'I may have said that.'

'But you're not missing it now, are you?'

'No, not exactly. I'm working.'

'Well, I want to work with you. To be together. That was what was wrong before. We came from separate worlds.'

'Of course we did.'

'You agree with me? That's fine.'

I thought of my world. According to the likes of my Uncle Arthur and Aunt Dot, a woman's place was in the kitchen or looking after the kids if there were any, not out robbing banks and building societies, blowing safes or holding up security guards.

'You see, it was like when I was being trained by SCRAP,' she said. 'We learnt all of what it was like trying to reform people, getting them cheap places to sleep and not very well-paid jobs. If you could do that you were a great success to SCRAP. They never taught us what it was like to live by stealing things. Nobody told us anything about the excitement.'

'I wish I never had.' I can't say I really approved of what was going on.

'No, Terry, I'm so glad you did. I feel we've come together. We can really bond.'

I didn't say anything to that, but she put her hand on mine on the table. I looked down at the greenish coin.

103

'What did you say this was exactly?'

'A Roman coin from the time of the Emperor Claudius. It was found in a field near St Albans.'

'What do you expect me to do with it?'

'Fence it,' she told me, 'through your usual chap. Where does he hang out?'

'Brighton,' I told her. She was getting to know some of the ropes already.

I had to pull out a number of tenners to pay the bill. Lucy watched me doing this and said, 'Ill-gotten gains!'

'What do you mean?'

'I expect everyone's paying with gains that are more or less ill-gotten. Faked expense accounts, pretending to be entertaining for business reasons, tax fiddles. It's just that yours are more openly ill-gotten, aren't they, darling?'

It was the first time anyone had called me that for years.

I took Lucy back to Notting Hill in a taxi. She seemed happy enough until we got to her flat, but she looked up and saw that the lights were on. Then she said, 'Oh damn!' and gave me a sort of fluttering kiss which just missed my mouth and landed on my nose. Then she jumped out of the taxi and ran away from me.

Lucy might have gone a long way to understand me, but she was still a bit of a puzzle so far as I was concerned. I felt in my pocket. The old green coin was still there.

14

It happened. It finally happened. And I must say it was a relief, although it's hard to explain and you probably won't understand unless you've done it yourself, which I don't for a second advise you to do, for reasons you'll discover before this story ends. What I have to do is tell you how this part of it began.

I've said how things began to go wrong, or right according to how you look at it, like when I began to have feelings for Terry which no praeceptor is meant to have for a client. Then I realized that I was shouting advice at him from another world entirely. In the world I came from, bishops and chaplains and praeceptors and probation officers, they all talked about sin and crime but they couldn't really understand anything about it. Take Robert, for instance. He preached hours and hours of sermons about sin, but I don't believe he'd ever committed the smallest sin in his life, not even been unfaithful to Sylvia, not even after she fell a victim to the G&Ts.

Orlando Wathen, Gwenny and Mr Markby all set themselves up as experts on crime, but, as Mr Wathen confessed, he couldn't understand the first thing about it. He hadn't had Terry explain the excitement. It was what turned a dull party at the Smith-Aldeneys into the most exciting turning point of my life.

When Christopher was showing me his collection, something he'd done many times before, the thought of doing it hadn't crossed my mind. It was when he was called away to get Sylvia a gin and left the Emperor Claudius out lying on the table that the sudden irresistible urge came over me. I suppose I could say it was all Sylvia's fault for wanting her own sort of drink that gave me the chance, but I won't. It was what Terry had told me and the sudden feeling of understanding him and being near him, closer to him than I could ever get in any other way. Oh well, I don't have to explain any more, do I? I felt everything had changed when I picked up the Claudius coin and put it in the back pocket of my jeans. So it was mine, and down in Aldershot they've never solved the mystery.

I know what you're going to say. You're going to say, 'What happened to that Lucinda Purefoy who wanted to do a bit of good in the world?' And I suppose I'd find that a hard one to answer, at least to your satisfaction. I suppose I might say that what I was doing was trying to do some good to Terry by understanding him and being on his side, and I think that's what I told myself. It sort of made sense to me at the time.

I tried to explain some of this to Terry. I wanted to get him to come out with me to some good, cheap place where we could eat dinner, but poor sweet, he insisted on taking me out to the most expensive restaurant in London run by the ghastly Jean Pierre O'Higgins, who does those wretched television programmes about how rude he has to be to the customers who criticize his awful cooking. The worst thing about it was that I had to pretend to be thrilled to be there and oooh and aaah over the crystallized seaweed with roasted p,té and oysters vinaigrette and the spiced cod in a veal sauce and, most horrible of all, the steak and kidney ice cream! It was at the end of this gastronomic nightmare that I did what I'd been longing to do. I produced the Emperor Claudius coin and told Terry I'd stolen it for him.

Honestly, I found his reaction disappointing. Let's say I'd expected more. I thought he might have congratulated me on what I'd done, although it couldn't possibly have been easier. I thought he might have welcomed me into his exciting world of thieves, where we could sink or swim together. I have to admit I felt really let down when he didn't welcome me into it at all.

Of course they'd warned us at SCRAP about this male chauvinist thing that criminals have, like they don't want women committing crimes, or sitting on juries or, especially, trying to reform them. Gwenny told us that was one of the hurdles we had to get over. It's the same thing again, isn't it? I mean, Tom Weatherby, soon to become my ex-boyfriend, for reasons I'll explain later, thinks that him writing scripts for documentaries no one in television seems to want is a serious business whereas my job in advertising at Pitcher's is just a sort of hobby, like Pilates classes or painting in watercolours. Robin Thirkell always thought my sincere ambition to do a bit of good in the world was a joke, and even my dad, for all his liberal views, seems a good deal more enthusiastic about gay marriages than he is about women bishops.

All I can say is that if being a woman is a hurdle in me getting closer to Terry, it's one I've got to get over as soon as possible.

In all this, Tom was no help at all.

I was particularly glad when Terry suggested

Thursday because that was when Tom planned to do some late-night research on his underground project and spend the night with his sister in Sidcup. So I thought the flat would be empty and I could invite Terry up after dinner, and cook him scrambled eggs if the food had been disgusting, or we could do whatever we wanted to do. I was sure he'd be in a pretty good mood after I'd shown my solidarity with him by handing over the coin. I was really angry with Tom when I found his plans had changed and all the lights were on in the flat when Terry took me home in a taxi. All we could manage was a quick frustrated kiss and then home. I suppose we could have gone on to the maisonette, but then I didn't fancy waking up to that crook and his awful secretary and, what's more, Terry never invited me.

Of course, Tom had some feeble excuse, it wasn't convenient for his sister to have him to stay, and nothing much was happening on the underground, as though that was a big surprise. Then he said, 'I suppose you wanted to bring the little thief up here?'

'Terry's not particularly little,' I reminded him.

'But he is a thief. I know you find that tremendously exciting. I'm terribly sorry. I do apologize! I've got no criminal convictions!'

I suppose if I'd listened to Tom at the time, I might have saved myself a great deal of trouble; but of course I didn't want to listen. All I knew was that our relationship, such as it was, had definitely fizzled out.

15

A few weeks went by after that dinner (I never dreamed seaweed could come so expensive), when I didn't see Lucy and I never rang her. I suppose I was a bit shocked when she told me she'd stolen something, like I was shocked when she told me to 'fuck off' all that time ago. Of course, you'll say I stole things and said fuck off, which is true, but it just didn't seem to me to be in Lucy's character. She'd shocked me again, I suppose that's what it was. For whatever reason, I never fenced that old green coin she gave me, but I kept it on the table by the side of my bed, to make sure she hadn't really become part of our business.

Which was growing all the time. I mean our business was. Chippy had taken on more part-time workers, who did the smaller odd jobs for us, and a character known as 'Screwtop Parkinson', who, Chippy said, drove a getaway car so fast no one would ever catch it. It may be that this talent came from the fact that he was slightly mad, as his name indicated, but Chippy said he could rely on Screwtop to get us out of any nasty situation and not stop to argue about the questions on *Who Wants to Be a Millionaire?*

Chippy, as head of a successful organization, was quite cheerful and continued to let me stay at the maisonette. He also told me what he thought was a good joke about another organization.

'They want me to be chairman of SCRAP. You know what that is, don't you, Terry?'

'Of course I know what it is.'

'They help young cons go straight. Do you think I'd be good at that?'

'I don't think you'd be good at it at all.'

Chippy gave me his one-sided smile. As I say, he was in a cheerful sort of a mood. 'Do you not?' he said. 'I think I know a good deal about young cons, like you yourself, Terry. Anyway, the lady from SCRAP's coming to call on me. She wants me to help in her drive for funding.'

'You mean she's coming here? To the maisonette?' I couldn't believe what I was hearing.

'I'll be concentrating on the environment that morning. I'll make sure all the criminal elements are out on business.'

That'll include me, I thought. I couldn't sit in the maisonette and tell some unknown woman that Chippy had persuaded me to choose the straight and narrow. I really couldn't. And then Chippy further amazed me by saying, 'Reckon if you do a job like that you get made a "sir" in the end. Play your cards right and you get knighted by the Queen.'

I couldn't get my mind round it and so I left Sir Leonard to his dreams.

*   *   *

I don't really know why but this chat with Chippy made me reluctant to ring Lucy. Although part of me wanted to, another part didn't want to have to tell her that her precious organization was going to be taken over by Sir Leonard 'Chippy' McGrath, one of the master blaggers of our times. So although my hand went to the phone in the maisonette from time to time, I didn't lift it up, as though it was something too hot to hold. But then, once again, everything changed.

It was a Sunday and I'd got up late. I was in my bedroom in the maisonette and I was wondering what I'd do that particular sunny morning, when I heard a furious hooting in the square below my window. I looked out and there she was, standing beside this clapped-out Polo, with her hand through the window beeping away on the horn.

'I ought to go down and see my dad,' she told me when I joined her in the square. 'And I thought we might have another picnic on the way down. Dad would be thrilled to see you.'

I told her I couldn't think why the bishop would want to see me at all.

'Because you're the one sinner that repented,' she told me. 'Of course we both know that you haven't repented at all, but we needn't tell Robert that. Hop in. We'll go and buy the picnic.'

She seemed very cheerful and as though she didn't expect any trouble from me. I had nothing much to look forward to except a long and boring Sunday with Sir Leonard in the maisonette. So I hopped in. We went round a Greek shop that was open in Queensway and bought kebabs and pitta bread, taramasalata and hummus and all that stuff including olives, all things Lucy knew about. Then we found an off-licence and got a bottle of Rioja like we'd had at our first picnic. Lucy said we were off to Folly Hill, where we went for the last picnic. 'But this one's going to be better than ever.'

So we got round the M25 and turned off down the M3 towards woods with spiky trees and sandy soil. Although I'd been driven by Lucy before, I hadn't remembered that the experience was, well,

I've got to admit, frightening. Lucy's idea of driving was to put her foot down on dangerous corners, although she did slow down a bit when the road was clear. When the road wasn't so clear she not only raced into corners but passed fast cars and lorries without any clear idea of what was going on ahead. I had to bite my tongue to stop myself saying, 'Hang about! You're not Screwtop Parkinson in the getaway car, let's go a bit slower and admire the scenery.' Of course, I didn't say this. I didn't want to spoil her day. All the same, I thought to myself, I'm the one who's meant to live dangerously with Leonard and his gang of blaggers, and yet Lucy's the one who's taking all the risks on the M3.

So it was a bit of a relief when we turned off on to the country roads and we got to this spot looking out over woods and fields. She parked the Polo not far from a farm gate and she set off, with a rug, plates and glasses. She called out at me to bring the lunch and follow her. What was she like? For a moment I remembered the way the screws would tell you to come out and take exercise, but I didn't mention that to Lucy. As I say, I didn't want to spoil her day.

Lucy had laid out the rug not far from the road, where an occasional car or a van did pass by. Once again it was her day and I didn't argue. I joined her and we sat down. I opened the Rioja and we took big swigs out of plastic cups and I agreed that the Arab stuff we bought tasted much better in the open air than marinated seaweed or whatever. The sun was shining and there was a bit of a breeze stirring the pointed trees and lifting Lucy's hair occasionally. She was smiling and laughing, chewing and gulping wine and looking happier, I thought, than at any time since we met.

When we'd finished eating Lucy produced another plastic bag from somewhere, this time it had 'Tesco' or 'Waitrose' written on it, I can't remember. It was heavy and clinked a bit as she handed it over to me with a big smile and she said, 'It's for you, Terry.'

I looked into it. Then I put the things out on the rug. I can't remember it all now, but there was a silver cigarette case, a couple of snuff boxes which I knew, from working with Chippy's experts, were quite valuable, an expensive Rolex watch, a gold pen and a pair of binoculars. It seemed to hurt her feelings when I laughed at this collection.

'Where the hell did you get this lot then?'

Lucy had stood up and was looking down at me and her collection, smiling proudly. 'Stuff I blagged. For you.'

'I told you I didn't want you to do that.'

'But I want to.' She was kneeling beside me now. 'You said it was exciting and it is. I could feel it. I could really understand.'

'It's different for me,' I told her. 'Quite different. I didn't need you to understand me.'

'But I want to, Terry. Don't you know how much I want to? You don't know how close I felt to you when I was doing it.'

Well, all I can say is that it didn't make me feel close to her. But she looked that much pleased with herself and proud of what she'd done, she seemed so bubbling over with it, that I just couldn't bring myself to say it. Anyway I'd explained it to her before, thieving is for men. They may do it to help their wives and their

113

girlfriends, I suppose, but they didn't need their help when they were working. And then, just when I was wondering whether it was right to call her a girlfriend, even in my head, I suddenly found her mouth was on my mouth and her fingers were after the zip in my trousers.

I'm sorry if you've been waiting for it, but I'm not going to describe what went on then in any sort of detail. The bits in the books I used to read in the Scrubs about sex were never very convincing and often quite embarrassing. I'd gone without sex anyway over those three and a bit years and managed to avoid the buggers on my particular landing.

When I got out, I couldn't break the habit of not doing it I'd got into in prison. I steered a bit clear of Diane, Leonard's secretary, although she made definite signals she was available. Then I met Lucy and after a bit of a rough time at first, when she wanted to change me into someone else, we began to get on together and her face hung about in my mind. Although I suppose I could have picked up some of the brass that hung around in the Beau Brummell Club, I didn't bother myself, and gradually it came over me that Lucy was the one I really fancied. I won't say that I didn't hope that something like this might happen when I got into the clapped-out Polo, but I wanted to make the suggestion and now there was obviously no need to do so.

So there we were together on the rug and occasionally I caught sight of the things she'd stolen, the gold pen and the binoculars, but I tried not to think about them. I heard a car stop and then go on again on the road above us, but after that, apart from the birds twittering in the pointed trees, everything was quiet.

That's really all that has to be said about it, except that when it was over I felt different. As though my prison days were well over.

16

Well, there it is. Thank goodness, it worked at last. I knew he didn't take it seriously when I gave him the Emperor Claudius coin. That could have been a bit of a joke after all. But then I showed him the things I'd picked up when some of us key workers were invited to dinner in Sir Carlton Pitcher's house in Regent's Park, and when Deirdre (you remember Deirdre? I was at school with her and she told me to join SCRAP) asked me and Tom Weatherby to dinner at her Uncle Charles's spread near Ascot. Well, I told her it had all fizzled out with me and Tom, and he'd moved back permanently to live with his sister in Sidcup. So I went alone. On my way to and from the loo, I managed to pick up quite a few items, including the snuff boxes I knew Terry would think had a bit of value to them.

In all this I was following the morality of the Youth Detention Centre and strictly confined myself to robbing from the rich without necessarily having to give to the poor. Well, as I say, I did get together these bits and pieces to show him, and I knew that was what I needed to bond with him.

Mind you, even at the start of the day, before I showed him the new stuff, he was nicer than he'd ever been. When I said hop in the car, he hopped. He helped me buy the picnic and he seemed really pleased to drive out into the wilds of Hampshire. Of course he sighed a bit and gripped his seat when I drove round corners, but all men do that because they think women can't drive. At least he didn't whimper, 'Please don't kill me,' like Tom Weatherby sometimes did. When I remember what Terry had been like when I first met him out of the Scrubs, the difference was extraordinary. We were no longer the reformer and the hard case. We were a criminally minded couple who more or less kept to the rules. The Emperor Claudius coin had, although I say it myself, paid its way.

Well, then I showed him the other things I blagged and I think he was pleased. What I hadn't quite thought through was what we should do once we'd bonded. I suppose I still thought that we might have a chance of reforming ourselves together. And then all that was put on hold, in a manner of speaking, because I took one look at him and you know what I said to myself, and this may surprise you, I said, 'Heathcliff.' Well, I knew he'd read *Wuthering Heights* in the Scrubs and I'd read it at school (another sort of a link between us) but there he was, my favourite character, who was irresistible but dangerous to know, sitting on the rug with the wind in his black curly hair, finishing off a chocolate bar, the spitting image of the love of Cathy's life and, well, mine too, by the way.

Of course you can guess what happened next. I really don't want to go into it, because although I think sex is great to do it's quite boring to read about it, more still to watch it in films or on the telly, with people's white bottoms going up and down to lots of overdone gasps and gurgling. All I can tell you is that we didn't do all that gasping and sound effects. In fact it all seemed wonderfully still and quiet round Folly Hill. I heard a car stop once and start again on the road above us, apart from that we bonded, Terry and I, in what seemed like a great quietness.

I'd promised Robert we'd have dinner at the palace (so called) before we drove back to London, and during the shepherd's pie (Dad and Mum have always been strong supporters of nursery food) my father came out with what I imagined was going to be his next 'Thought for the Day' on Radio 4.

'God gave the joy of sex,' he said, shaking the tomato ketchup bottle sharply over his shepherd's pie, 'to our forefather and mother in his garden of Eden. We must assume from all we can read in the book of Genesis that our common ancestors enjoyed the heavenly gift of coitus in the open air.'

'Why?' Terry asked in surprise, a forkful of potato about to enter his mouth.

'Why what?' Robert said tolerantly, only a little impatiently at the interruption.

'Why must we assume that it took place in the open air?'

'Well, that's a very good question.' I thought my dad sounded a bit patronizing at this point. 'I'm glad you asked me that intelligent question, Terry. Because we don't read of Adam and Eve having built any sort of home or indeed shelter in the garden. We must assume that the climate was always favourable in those far-off days.' Robert's thoughts seemed to me to be getting a little too close for comfort. 'I said that to Charlie Fawcett today. We'd met at an inter-diocesan conference on "Spreading the Word" in Basingstoke and I was giving him a lift back to his Farnham rectory and we'd just got to Folly Hill when he suddenly said, "Stop the car!" I thought he'd heard the exhaust

118

drop off or something so I stopped, but all Charlie said was, "Look at that! Isn't it disgusting?" Well, I looked down from the road and all I could see was a couple stretched out on a rug apparently enjoying God's great gift of sexual intercourse al fresco under the arch of heaven.'

'Did you see who they were?' I had to ask him.

'Certainly not! I just took a quick look and drove on, but Charlie Fawcett went on and on about people using the English countryside as though it were their own private bedroom. And he talked about some white bottom going up and down. He said it was disgusting.'

I looked at Terry. He was chomping away without any expression at all. So it was left to me to say, 'Disgusting!' as though Charlie Fawcett had a point. Of course it was quite disgusting, but wonderful as well.

'So, no one need be ashamed.' Robert was completing his 'Thought' of enjoying the gift God has given us in all weathers.

Sylvia, who'd brought her gin and tonic into dinner, made no comment. I wondered if she and Robert had ever done it 'al fresco', but then quickly dismissed the idea from my mind.

17

'Quite honestly, I'm worried about her. Seriously worried.'

'And she is. . . ?'

'My good friend.' After the picnic I felt I was justified in calling Lucy that.

'And what is it that worries you about her exactly? Has she got what I suppose you'd call "a bun in the oven"?'

Mr Markby gave me a rare Scottish sort of a smile which flickered only for a moment.

'No, it's not that.'

'What is it then?'

'It's her thieving.' I'd taken a deep breath and told him. 'I'm worried about her thieving.'

I'd called to make my routine visit to my probation officer. I sat opposite him and we talked across the desk in a cold office with a big filing cabinet, a pot plant that looked as if it hadn't got long to live and, on his desk, a framed photograph of a determined-looking woman and a cross-looking small boy who was a Markby lookalike without, of course, the moustache.

As you know, I never liked Mr Markby, not since he robbed me of my parole, but I was stuck for someone to come to for advice and the fact I'd come to him seemed to be an unexpected point in my favour.

'You're worried about your friend's thieving and you've come to tell me about it?'

'I didn't know who else I could tell.'

'Quite right, come to the professional. I don't

suppose that girl from SCRAP's any help at all in this situation.'

'I'm afraid she's not.'

'Just as I thought. Now, let's see.' He turned over his notes. 'You're still living in Leonard McGrath's accommodation?'

'I'm still in the maisonette, yes.'

'And working for Environmentally Friendly Investments?' Mr Markby sounded far more friendly than usual.

'I'm still working with him, yes.'

'He's a good man, Terry. He's been a good man to you.' Mr Markby was looking extremely serious, and I did my best to give him a serious look back.

'He's been a help to me.'

'A force for good in the world. Gwendolen Gerdon was looking for a new chairman and I gave her Leonard McGrath's name. I told her he'd shake the SCRAP organization up a bit. Don't you think so?' Mr Markby's shoulders were now shaking as though he found this funny, although he had no idea how funny it really was. Then his shoulders calmed down as he said, 'You're really concerned about this friend of yours, aren't you?'

'Most concerned.' I really was.

'That shows how much the Probation Service has done for you. You were a comparatively young offender?'

'Since I was a kid.'

'Since childhood, yes. And now you're genuinely concerned about your friend. What does she steal, by the way?'

'Bits and pieces. Old coins. A gold pen. Snuff boxes she got. They might be worth a bit actually. Sort of glasses you take out racing, a good watch.'

'The menopause?'

'What?'

'It happens to women of a certain age. Is she of a certain age, by any chance?'

'Twenty-three.'

'Then the menopause has got nothing to do with it. Nor has kleptomania. I don't call it an illness, Terry. Just plain, simple crime. And greed. That's what it was, wasn't it, Terry, when you used to do it yourself?'

'When I used to do it, yes.'

'Well, you can point this out to her. Where did it get you, all that thieving you did? Into prison for a long time, that's where it got you.'

'Got me in for a much longer time because of you,' was what I didn't say. Instead I told him, 'I'll try all that.'

'Yes, you try all that. Make her think about it seriously. Really scare her. Tell her she wouldn't enjoy Holloway, would she?'

'I don't think so.'

'I don't think so either. Be gentle with her of course. Gentle and understanding. But be perfectly clear. She's committing crimes and she'll end up in prison. Will you do that?'

'I'll certainly try it.'

'Tell her that if you could give up stealing which had been going on since you were a young child, surely she can.'

I didn't say I'd told Lucy that. I didn't make any promises.

'Oh, and stay close to her. Keep an eye on her. If she's going to go straight and resist the temptation to steal things, she'll need continued support.'

'I'll remember that,' I told him.

Then he looked at me, sort of sizing me up. 'I don't suppose,' he said, 'you've ever thought of joining the Probation Service, have you?'

I could quite honestly tell him that I hadn't.

'Pity,' he said. 'We could do with lads like you.'

*   *   *

Because Mr Markby had told me to keep an eye on Lucy, I agreed to move in to her flat in Notting Hill Gate. Anyway, I'd got a bit tired of the maisonette, what with Diane's long suggestive looks and the future Sir Leonard 'Chippy' McGrath becoming more and more pompous after his name had been mentioned as the possible future chairman of SCRAP.

In the flat (All Saints Road, up a couple of floors) I could still go out on any of the big jobs when Chippy needed my help. Apart from that, I saw that Lucy got up in time for work and left thieving to the professionals. During the day I did the shopping, cleaned up and read some of the books Lucy had on the shelves in the lounge. In the evenings, Lucy either got me cooking with her or we went out locally for a Chinese or an Indian. Looking back, it was about the best time of my life, but nothing much happened in the story I've got to tell. Except perhaps I ought to just mention the evening Lucy said she was getting a bit bored with the Beau Brummell and she'd take me to 'her club', which was the Close-Up in Soho. Anyway, she said it was her club but it seemed that her ex, Tom Weatherby, was the member and she told the girl on the desk we were waiting for him, which of

123

course we weren't.

'Well, well, I see you've got a new friend.' A tall woman with a sort of commanding voice, bright red hair and permanently raised eyebrows came straight up to us with her hands in the pockets of her floppy trousers. She was with a thick-set, grinning man who I put down as Caribbean. Lucy said, 'This is Deirdre,' and told her that I was her new friend, Terry Keegan. Then Deirdre asked if Lucy had picked me up at SCRAP. When Lucy admitted it, Deirdre said that was where she'd picked up Ishmael. She seemed very proud of him. 'He's a terrific rap singer, you know.'

Then Deirdre went on to tell us that after the dinner at her Uncle Charles's spread it was discovered that a few little things were missing, including two or three of his precious snuff boxes. The funny thing was that Deirdre's uncle suspected Ishmael, although he was busy entertaining them all with his rap and never went off around the house on his own. They still suspected him—pure bloody racism.

'How ridiculous!' Lucy was saying, cool as a cold beer. At which little Ishmael started laughing until he shook all over. 'Yes, it was. Very ridiculous!' he managed to splutter out through his laughter.

I thought that another reason why Lucy should stop thieving was that professional blaggers like this Ishmael shouldn't get blamed for all the crimes she committed.

18

EXTRACT FROM THE MINUTES OF THE
COUNCIL,
SOCIAL CARERS, REFORMERS AND
PRAECEPTORS
Meeting held at SCRAP offices, King's Cross

Present:

GWENDOLEN GERDON, Executive Director
(ED)
LADY DOUGHBERRY, representing the
Bunyan Society for Prison Reform
PROFESSOR MAXWELL HEATHERINGTON,
Reader in Criminology at the University of East
Surrey
CAMPBELL DYSON, Chair of Dyson Soft
Furnishing
IVY SINCLAIR, BBC *Today* programme
PETER BETHELL, partner in the firm of Bethell,
Sherman and Pensotti, Solicitors
THE REV. HARVEY TYLER, Rector, St
Barnabas, King's Cross
ALEX MARKBY, representing the Probation
Service
LEONARD MCGRATH, Chair of
Environmentally Friendly Investments

The ED told the meeting that they all very much
regretted that Orlando Wathen, after many years
of distinguished service as chair of SCRAP, had

tendered his resignation as his views on the treatment of offenders had changed considerably and he no longer felt comfortable with our standpoint on crime and the reform of criminals.

Peter Bethell told the meeting that as Orlando's close friend and legal adviser he knew that Orlando was sad to leave but that he had, in all honesty, to make way for a chair who would share the traditional SCRAP belief in the seed of essential good, in even the worst offender, which could be nurtured and nourished.

Lady Doughberry wished her regret at Mr Wathen's new stance to be minuted but proposed a vote of thanks to him and SCRAP's best wishes for his many years of service. Peter Bethell seconded and the motion was carried nem. con.

The ED then told the meeting that in casting round to find a suitable successor as chair we were grateful to Alex Markby, representing the Probation Service, for his kind assistance. He had a proposal to put before the council.

Alex Markby told the meeting that, given the recent report on the organization's finances, he felt SCRAP stood in need of a well-known businessman who would have experience of fund-raising to work with Campbell Dyson on the money side. He had been recently most impressed by the generosity of Leonard McGrath, the head of the well-known firm Environmentally Friendly Investments. Leonard had given a job to a young man, Terry Keegan, recently out of the Scrubs, and even put him up in his own maisonette. Alex Markby said he didn't want to dismiss the well-intentioned efforts of the girl Lucy Purefoy from SCRAP who was in charge of Terry Keegan's case, but he wasn't convinced that she took her work entirely seriously. On one occasion, she had misinformed him about Keegan's address; she seemed to imagine he was working on some sort of farm in the country when he was in fact being cared for and housed by Leonard McGrath, who had become his true praeceptor, counsellor and friend. In his (Alex Markby's) view, Leonard McGrath would make a perfect chair for SCRAP and 'would raise our profile in the business world'. He said that Mr McGrath was prepared to say a few words.

Leonard McGrath said he felt that the time had come for him to 'give back to society something he had taken out of it' and he looked forward to doing his best for SCRAP. In a long business career he had always taken a considerable interest in the causes of crime and in particular in young criminals. He had been pleased to give shelter to Terry Keegan when he came out of prison and delighted that this young man was now in regular employment. If he was to be offered the chair, he could 'only say I'll do my best'.

Alex Markby proposed and Peter Bethell seconded 'that Leonard McGrath should be appointed chair of SCRAP'. The proposal was passed nem. con.

There was no other business so the meeting ended and tea was served at 4.45 p.m.

19

'It's in the *Guardian*,' I told Terry at breakfast. 'Leonard McGrath made chairman of SCRAP. That couldn't be anything to do with your friend in the maisonette, could it?'

'It *is* my friend in the maisonette—Chippy reckons he's in with the chance of a knighthood.' Terry was buttering toast. He wasn't laughing. He had told me all about his old friend Chippy McGrath, who had managed to follow a career in crime without ever being caught and had now emerged as Leonard McGrath, head of the organization for which Terry worked at nights, head of Environmentally Friendly Investments and now of SCRAP.

'But that's ridiculous!' I said.

'Yes, it is. Very ridiculous.' But he still wasn't laughing.

'Do you think SCRAP ought to be told?'

'I don't think Chippy would like that.'

'I suppose we needn't take SCRAP seriously any more,' I suggested.

'No, we needn't take it seriously.'

This was a kind of relief, but then Terry changed the subject. He said he'd been to see Mr Markby, his probation officer.

'Routine visit?' Quite honestly, I didn't have a whole lot of time for Mr Markby.

'Not quite routine.' Terry looked unusually serious. 'I told him how worried I am.'

'I think life's taken a distinct turn for the better.' I poured more coffee. 'What are you worried about?'

'You.'

'What?'

'I told him I was worried about you. Of course, I didn't say you by name. I called you a friend.'

'Well, I certainly am that.' I could have said I was a friend who didn't want to be discussed with Mr Markby.

'I said I'd got a friend who'd taken to thieving.'

'I think you've got lots of friends who've taken to thieving.'

'I said it was my girlfriend. He advised me to tell you that it would land you up in prison like it did me.'

'But you explained it to me. Isn't that why it's so exciting? The risk, I mean.'

'I don't want you to take no risks, Lucy.'

'Why not? I'm not objecting to you taking risks. Not at the moment anyway.'

'I'm different,' Terry said. 'Completely different.'

'Because you're a man?' I'd got Terry cooking but I still couldn't get rid of the male chauvinist side of him. I was pretty irritated by the fact that he'd looked at the things I'd managed to steal lately with something like contempt.

'Not that I'm a man, Lucy. Because I grew up to it. And because I do the big, serious jobs. The bits and pieces you bring home aren't either here or there.'

'Not even the snuff boxes?'

'Well, the snuff boxes might bring in a bob or two,' he had to admit.

'Stop doing that male superiority thing then. Anyway, you know I'm only doing it to understand

129

you. To be near to you. To be at one with you. You know that, don't you, Terry?' I don't think I could have put it more nicely. But I was not altogether pleased by his reply.

'You'll never be like me because you don't do serious jobs. It's just a sort of game to you, isn't it, Lucy? But it's not to me. It's how I earn a living. That's why I want you to stop doing it.'

'You mean you want to reform me.' I'm afraid I rather snapped at him.

'Something like that, I suppose,' he had to admit. So then I left him to put the dishes in the washing machine and went to work.

When I came back that evening I dialled 1571 for my messages and immediately got the high-pitched sound of Robin Thirkell, a voice which would make you think he was gay if you didn't happen to know, as I did, that he was rather a shady form of heterosexual.

'Lucy, darling!' Robin was carolling down the line. 'I'm inviting you to no end of champagne and caviar and I hope it's going to be an amusing evening. Come alone, if you don't mind. I really want to enjoy your company far away from that tedious little criminal who pissed off out of the Intimate without a single word to me, darling, despite all I'd done for him. It would be the loveliest thing if you could arrive at God's Acre around 7.30 Saturday. See you then, darling. I'm so excited.'

I pressed three to erase the call and when Terry came home I told him that Robin had invited me to a rather grand dinner party in the country. 'But you'll probably be too busy to come.' I didn't bother to tell him that the invitation was only for me, because I knew he wouldn't fancy it anyway.

'Yes,' Terry said, 'I probably will be busy.'

After that he cooked supper and we watched something unwatchable on the television.

*   *   *

When I drove into the yard of God's Acre that Saturday at 7.30, Robin's Mercedes and his Range Rover were littered about the place but I saw no other cars. I knew that Robert and Sylvia hadn't been invited but I didn't know who had, or where they might have got to. As I climbed out of the Polo I got the usual long hysterical barks from the four bull terriers, who bared their teeth and seemed about to attack me until I called them by their names, Judy, Greta, Marlene and Virginia, then they calmed down, started licking my hands and had to be shoved away when I reached the front door.

The door was opened by Max, Robin's sort of butler, who wore a short white jacket which was never entirely clean and showed the ends of his braces. Max had ginger hair and had never shaved adequately at the top of his cheekbones. 'His nibs is in the living room, Lucy,' he told me, then returned to the kitchen, to finish the large whisky he'd no doubt been drinking before I rang the front-door bell.

Robin had done up God's Acre Manor like a homage to Cecil Beaton. There were a lot of heavy curtains held back by ties with massive gold tassels, statues of marble cherubs and black boys on marble columns and a selection of gold-framed photographs on top of the grand piano, many of

131

them of Robin as a winsome child. There was a smell of lime-and-lemon-flavoured air freshener mixed with a whiff of incense, and Frank Sinatra was singing 'Fly Me to the Moon' on the hi-fi. I remembered a time when I found Robin's decor rather grand and exciting, but that was before I met Terry. Now I thought it just poncey.

'Where's the party?' I asked him.

'There isn't a party. Just me.' Robin was wearing a blue velvet smoking-jacket thing and offering me strips of toast with caviar on them.

'But you said . . .'

'What's it matter what I said?' He gave me that roguish little-boy look that I now found mildly irritating.

'So why did you say it?'

'Well, I thought you wouldn't come if it was just me. Isn't that true? Not now you've taken to rough trade from Her Majesty's prisons.'

'I can't stay tonight,' I told him quite firmly.

'What a pity! Got to get back to tempting little Terry, have you?'

'Yes,' I told him, 'I've got to get back.' At which he said nothing but offered me some more caviar and quail's eggs, and that was just for starters.

We were soon alone in the dining room, being served by Max, who winked at me over the roast pheasant as though he knew exactly what I'd come for. I was almost moved to shout at him, 'I'm going home tonight!' But then Robin was being quite bitchily funny about all the neighbours, so I decided to ignore Max and merely disappoint his expectations later. Towards the end of dinner, when I'd had the champagne and a good deal of red wine, Robin suddenly said, 'I've got a

Bonnard.'

Now, quite honestly, you'll have to excuse me. I'm not really up in the world of art. At that time I didn't know what a Bonnard was. It might have been a brand of dog, or a vintage car, or a type of Italian suit. Then Robin said, 'My Uncle Everard left it to me in his will.'

'That was nice of him, I suppose.' Really I had no idea whether it was or not.

'He wasn't really my uncle, of course. Everard Egglington. He was a close friend of my mother. We always called him "uncle". An old queen who'd made pots of money out of Egglington cigarettes and ran this art gallery as a kind of hobby. I know he fancied me when I was young but he never got to first base. All the same he left me this wonderful picture. You should see it.'

'I'd like to.'

'After dinner?'

Well, of course, after dinner it became clear that the great Bonnard picture was upstairs and, of course, in his bedroom. However, I felt so completely attached to Terry and so confident of my powers of refusal that I let Robin take me into the familiar room with the big four-poster bed with carved wooden leaves at the top of each column and a shield on the crossbar with some sort of coat of arms which was certainly not Robin's.

But there was something new. There on the wall a slim, pinkish youngish woman was drying her thighs near a big white bathtub. She looked utterly uninterested in what was going on anywhere else in the world, totally absorbed in what she was doing. I rather envied her.

'I like it,' I told Robin. I really did.

133

'I like it too. Of course she's not *in* the bath. It would go for millions if Mrs Bonnard was in the bath. But that little thing's worth 400,000.'

'Really?' My interest in the picture increased.

'That's what the gallery told me.'

I examined Robin's 'little Bonnard' more closely, and I asked him if he wasn't afraid of burglars.

'Not a bit. The dogs would just fly at anyone they didn't know. They'd wake up Max and he's a match for any burglar.'

'Why do you keep it up here?'

'Oh, I'll find a place for it downstairs some time. Meanwhile I like to wake up and gloat over it. And last thing at night I remind myself I've got it. Shall we go to bed now?'

'Go to bed? Whatever for?' I asked him, looking innocent, although I knew perfectly well.

'Sex, of course. With all the trimmings.'

I remembered what the trimmings were with Robin and knew I no longer wanted them.

'I don't think so.'

'Are you turning me down?'

'Flat!'

Robin looked thoughtful and then said casually, 'What did you do with the Emperor Claudius coin?'

'I don't know what you mean.'

'Oh yes, you do. What did you do with Christopher Smith-Aldeney's Emperor Claudius coin after you put it in your back pocket?'

'I still don't know what you mean.'

'I mean either we go to bed now or I tell the neighbourhood, including the dear bishop.'

'That's blackmail.' I was profoundly shocked.

134

'It's a crime.'

'I know it is. Almost as bad a crime as thieving.'

'You can tell who you like,' I told him. 'I'll deny it and no one's going to believe you.'

'Let's stop talking.' Robin had given up the threats for the moment and turned on the charm. His shirt was now wide open, his face lit up with a smile. 'Hop into bed, why don't you? You know you want to.'

I was up against the wall as he tried to embrace me. I felt his arm round me and the overpowering smell of his Roger et Gallet eau-de-Cologne. All I could do was to bring my knee up smartly, a gesture met with a cry of pain. I did win the fifty-yard sprint at school and, in less time than it takes to tell, I was out of the house, across the yard (I didn't even have time to call the dogs by their names) and in the Polo. Luckily the key was still in the ignition and I left God's Acre at around sixty miles an hour.

On the way home I drove along Folly Hill. It was then I remembered how good life could sometimes be. I was also thinking about a picture worth £400,000.

20

I didn't think I was getting anywhere. Mr Markby didn't seem to want to have a word with Lucy. Nothing I said to her about the danger of ending up inside stopped her from lifting small bits and pieces of other people's property and giving them to me, with the sort of proud look I used to see on my Aunt Dot's cat when it brought in a dead bird and laid it on the carpet.

Whenever I told Lucy what I thought about it she said she was doing it for my sake 'so we could share a common experience'. I tried to tell her that we weren't really sharing anything. What I did was serious business which brought in a decent wage that paid the rent and would take us on holiday to Ibiza later, while what she did wouldn't keep us in hot dinners. She just went away with a smile and stopped listening. It seemed to me I only had one place to go and there was only one person who might have a bit of clout with Lucy. She went to work on the bus every day, having nowhere to park in Oxford Street, so I took the Polo from its resident's parking place and headed off in the direction of Aldershot.

I found Lucy's mum in the palace, about one of the smallest palaces in the country I'd say, wandering vaguely from room to room, but when she asked me to join her in a 'snifter' I had to refuse politely and ask where my girlfriend's dad might be found. It turned out he was in the cathedral, preparing for a special service on 'Family Values' to be broadcast over the radio next Sunday.

I'd never been in a cathedral before, never much in a church if it comes to that. The one in Aldershot seemed to be very cold and grey and there were rows and rows of empty chairs. Around the walls were statues of dead people lying on marble boxes with their legs crossed, sometimes with their feet on little dogs. Up at the far end there were lights and a bit of activity. Some man was fixing up a mike and others were having a conversation. An organ somewhere stopped and started and a row of young kids was going through a song, over and over and bit by bit in a way which would drive you bananas if you had to listen to it too long.

I stood blinking in the shadows for a minute and then I spotted Lucy's dad in the back row of the chairs. He was wearing a sort of long black skirt arrangement and scribbling away in a notebook as though there was no tomorrow.

'Terry!' I have to say he gave me a great welcome as I made my way towards him down a row of empty chairs. 'You've come to church! There's more joy in heaven over one sinner that repenteth—well, I've told you that before, haven't I?'

'Actually I haven't come to church.'

'You've come to cathedral. It's just another house of God. What's the matter? Are you afflicted by any sort of doubt?'

He was smiling a lot, a good-looking older guy with very white teeth and a strong smell of aftershave.

'I haven't come to church really,' I said. 'I just wanted to find you.'

137

'And here I am.' The bishop spread out his arms as though he'd performed some sort of miracle just by being there. 'With God's help I'm here for you today, Terry. What's your trouble?'

'It's not my trouble exactly. It's your daughter's.'

'You mean Lucy?'

'Yes, I do mean Lucy.'

'What sort of trouble? Overdrawn at the bank? Can't find the rent? Lucy's always been a little vague about money.'

'She's not vague about it now. In fact she's been stealing some of it.'

'Whatever do you mean?' He was still smiling, as though I'd made a joke.

'Money and other things. Snuff boxes. Bits of silver. One time it was a pair of binoculars. That's what I came to tell you, Mr Purefoy.'

'Bishop Purefoy.'

'Sorry.'

'It doesn't really matter. Now what is it you're trying to tell me?'

'That your daughter's a thief, Bishop Purefoy.'

'How very interesting.' He uncrossed his legs and leaned forward as though he didn't want to miss a word of what I was saying.

'She steals things and I'm afraid she's going to get caught because she's had no training.'

'And you say she's just started.'

'Just recently, yes.'

'Classic!' he said. 'It's a classic situation!'

'You mean a lot of bishops have thieving daughters?'

'No. Not that. Not that at all. God sent Jesus down to redeem our sins and then sent Freud down to explain them. Oh, I'm sorry,' Lucy's dad seemed suddenly embarrassed, 'I don't suppose you know much about Freud!'

As a matter of fact he was wrong. Not having spent what seemed like years in a cell reading books, he made the usual mistake of thinking I didn't know much about anything. I knew enough about Freud to be sure he had nothing to do with our present discussion. All I said was, 'I don't think it takes much explaining.'

'Oh yes, it does. You see, you're the thief, Terry.'

'I've got to admit that.' I didn't want to go into further detail.

'You're the thief and not Lucy.'

'Me *and* Lucy. I just told you.'

'You told me because that's what you want to believe. You probably need to.'

'I don't want to believe it. In fact I'd far rather not believe it.'

'You'd rather not have it, this guilt. So of course this is where our old friend Freud comes in.'

Freud, I thought, was no old friend of mine and I only wished he'd keep out of it. But I couldn't stop the bishop, who was now rubbing his knees in excitement.

'It's a classic case! The transference of guilt!'

'Transference of *what*?'

'You don't like your guilt. That's all perfectly natural. Guilt's not a very nice thing to have. Like gastric flu or sciatica. Anyway, you don't want your guilt, of course you don't, so you hand it on to my daughter.'

'But I came down here to see you. So you could help. Isn't that what they're there for, bishops?'

'Of course you need help and I'm going to help

you, Terry. Claude Dauncey, author of *God on the Psychiatrist's Couch*, lives in Guildford. Brilliant man! You can mention my name when you ask for an appointment.'

There was a burst of music and the kids up by the altar started singing again. The bishop stood and told me, 'Robin Thirkell came to see me with some ridiculous story about Lucy stealing old coins from Christopher Smith-Aldeney. No doubt you'd been spreading rumours. My advice to you, Terry, is to keep your guilt to yourself. Oh, and get an urgent appointment with Claude Dauncey. Now I must go and see to our "Family Values" special service. Next Sunday on Radio 4, if you happen to be listening. It's all God's work.'

After he'd gone I sat for a while looking at the grey walls and marble boxes full of old bones. I thought that Lucy's dad knew a good deal about Freud and God, but he didn't seem to have much understanding of his daughter.

21

He told me he'd been down to see my dad about reforming me and of course I was furious. I remembered how far apart we'd been when I was trying to be the reformer, and how much he'd hated me for it. Dad, being Dad, hadn't taken much notice of what Terry told him and came out with some wild idea about the transference of guilt which gave him the comfort of believing that his one and only daughter couldn't possibly have taken up the habit of nicking small objects of value from other people's homes. I didn't want to disillusion Dad any more than I'd have whispered in his ear, 'There's no one upstairs!' just as he was putting on his mitre.

But something had to be done about it and it was at this time, i.e. very soon after my rapid flight from Robin Thirkell's bedroom, that I had what I called 'the Great Idea'.

The more I thought about the idea the greater it became. At least it would wipe off that patronizing, worried little smile that arrived far too often on Terry's face. At best it would bind us together for always, equals with a full understanding of each other. We'd be real partners, and not that come-and-go sort of partner people like Deirdre call whoever they happen to be sleeping with at the time.

Speaking of Deirdre, she still phoned me at work from time to time. When Terry was out one evening on business he wasn't going to tell me about (well, when I got the Great Idea going, all

141

that would have to change) I promised to meet her again for a drink after work in the Close-Up Club.

So there she was as usual, looking extremely pleased with herself, together with Ishmael, who had entertained the dinner guests at her Uncle Charles's spread in Ascot with some of his more outrageous rap while I knocked off a few articles. We sat at the bar fingering our glasses of white wine and all around us people were greeting each other with loud cries of 'Hi!' and boasting of astonishing film and television deals which would probably never come off.

'Hello, praeceptor!' Deirdre had greeted me. 'How's the little crook you're busy turning into a little angel?'

'I'm not a praeceptor any more actually.' I had to say I was a bit miffed by her tone of voice. 'And Terry's certainly not an angel. He's moved in with me now.'

'Terry Keegan has moved in with you?' Come to think of it, it was almost the first time that the rap singer had spoken directly to me. He either sat in silence or burst into songs which were most likely to offend. So his sudden interest surprised me.

'Why? Do you know Terry Keegan?' I asked him. For an answer Ishmael took a big gulp of white wine and muttered, 'I may have heard of him.' I suppose that in the underworld Ishmael inhabited quite a lot of people would have heard of Terry.

'It's a great relief he's moved in,' I told them. 'Terry's a good cook, so we don't have to go to ridiculously expensive restaurants or that awful Beau Brummell Club he belongs to.'

'Ah yes.' Ishmael was nodding away, still smiling.

'I know a few people who are members of that club.'

He was still nodding, apparently wisely, when Deirdre said, 'You remember that Gwenny told us never to sleep with anyone we met through SCRAP?'

'She said it would have disastrous results,' I agreed. 'But it hasn't, has it?'

'Not so far!' the suddenly loquacious rap artist cheerfully agreed. And then he ordered another bottle of New Zealand Chardonnay. It was an evening full of surprises.

When we got down to the end of the bottle, I heard myself say to Deirdre, 'It's a problem, isn't it? We come from such different worlds, Terry and me and you and Ishmael. Don't you find it difficult to, well, sort of bridge the gap?'

'Not really.' Deirdre would never admit that there was anything the slightest bit difficult about her perfect existence. 'Do you find it difficult to get close to Terry?'

'Of course we're close,' I couldn't help saying. 'But I've got a great idea about how to get even closer. I mean, I want to understand exactly how he feels. I want to be part of his life. Not some superior sort of reformer.'

'Really?' The rap singer looked at me, apparently fascinated. 'And we'd be so very interested to hear what that great idea is.'

'I might tell you when it's all over,' was all I could say. 'On the other hand, I might not.' I raised my glass and drank a discreet toast to the future.

*   *   *

It's no good thinking now of what my Great Idea led to or all its results which I didn't even consider at the time. I have to think myself back to when the Great Idea filled up my mind and I got more and more excited about it. I also found it exciting to keep it a secret from Terry, as though it was something special I was buying him for Christmas or his birthday, and I was saving it up as a huge surprise.

My first thought in the early days of the Great Idea was to get myself really fit for the experience. Terry had talked about things like sky-diving, so I realized I had to go into training. I spent a lot of time in the Lysander Club, which I'd joined but only used to go to occasionally for a swim. I was a regular at the aerobics class, where the loud-voiced girl with the cropped top and the microphone fixed to her head shouted, 'Tits, bums, stomachs, squeeze now, squeeze!' her voice rising high above the dance music. There was I, working away in Lycra leggings, perfecting my core stability and doing cardiovascular exercises to make sure my heart was in the right place and strong enough to put the Great Idea into practice.

At times an older, more serious woman arrived at the Lysander to give us Pilates lessons. So we stretched our legs in sort of elastic bands and my core stability became amazing and my legs, which I might have to depend on, were in first-rate condition. Terry wasn't best pleased that I was spending so many evenings at the Lysander, but then, as I say, he had no idea that I was doing it entirely for him.

When I felt fit and ready, I rang the SCRAP

office and asked Gwenny if I could speak to Leonard McGrath. I did this because I didn't want to meet him at the Connaught Square maisonette, where my Great Idea would get known to everyone, including the ghastly secretary and, no doubt, eventually Terry.

'You want to speak to our chair?'

'If your chair happens to be around.'

'Leonard's extremely generous with his time.'

'I'm sure he is.'

'He gives us an hour and a half at lunchtime on Thursdays. We get through more work with him than Orlando seemed to manage all week.'

'I'll call in on Thursday then.'

'Can I help? I mean, it must be about young Terry. Is he in trouble again?'

'Not at all. So far as I know.'

'You've managed to find him accommodation?'

'Oh yes. I got him settled in a flat in Notting Hill Gate.'

'Well done! And is he working?'

'Regularly. Mainly at nights.'

'Well, I suppose that pays better than day work.'

'Yes, it seems to.'

You see how confident I'd become since I had the idea? When I got to the SCRAP office early in my Thursday lunch hour I marched straight across to Orlando Wathen's old room and into it in spite of Gwenny's protests.

The new chair was munching a sandwich, washing it down with a gulp of white wine and reading some no doubt boring SCRAP report.

As he looked up at me I closed the door behind me and said, quite clearly, 'Chippy, they say you're doing a marvellous job at SCRAP.'

145

He looked at me, clearly furious. He had his jacket off and I could see his distended stomach and, as I looked down on him, the bald patch in his hair. He'd kept out of prison, but I thought Terry had preserved his looks far better. 'Don't you ever call me that in here,' he said in a furious whisper. 'Don't you *ever* call me that in here.'

'Why not? I can't wait to tell Gwenny that you planned the jobs Terry went to prison for. Of course, I might keep calling you "Leonard" if you'll cooperate with me.'

'What's that mean? Money?'

'Not at all. Just your help and the help of your other organization.' By this time I was sitting comfortably down beside the new chair.

'What for? Something to do with Terry?'

'Eventually perhaps. What I want your help for has more to do with Bonnard.'

'Bonnard?' Chippy was momentarily puzzled.

'French painter,' I explained.

Chippy supplied the rest. 'Influenced by Gauguin and Van Gogh,' he said. 'Founded the Salon d'Automne.'

'You studied History of Art?' I remembered people who had done that subject at Manchester. They weren't in the least like Chippy. But he had now gone back to being Leonard McGrath, chair of SCRAP and distinguished private collector.

'My art expert and I,' he explained, with his curious little twisted smile, 'have been on the lookout for a Bonnard.'

'He painted a picture of a naked woman standing beside a bath and drying her thighs.'

'That would be his wife, Marthe,' Chippy told me. 'He painted her lots of times, in and out of the

146

bath. She was his favourite subject.'

'So how much do you think a painting of Marthe might be worth?'

'In or out of the bath?'

'I told you. Out of it.'

His fingers drummed on his desk. He pursed his lips and looked thoughtful.

'The dealer said 400,000,' I told him.

Chippy looked impressed. 'Is it in good condition?'

'Perfect!' Of course I didn't really know whether it was or not.

'I suppose it's locked up in some museum or other?' Chippy said after more thought.

'No,' I told him. 'It's hanging on a nail on someone's bedroom wall.'

And it was then, of course, I told him my Great Idea and he promised his full cooperation.

On my way out, Gwenny looked up at me expectantly from her desk and asked if I'd had a good meeting with Chair.

'Yes,' I said. 'It was an excellent meeting!'

'And did he help you with Terry?'

'Oh yes,' I told her. 'He was a considerable help with Terry.'

After work I knew that Terry was busy and out for the evening, so I went for a swim and a cranial massage. I was on my way across the gym to get an organic cheese and beetroot sandwich and have a read of the newspaper when I passed a familiar figure on the stationary bicycle which you have to pedal very hard to get nowhere.

'Ishmael,' I said. 'I didn't know you'd joined the Lysander Club.'

'Oh yes.' He gave me one of his sweetest smiles.

'You have to keep fit in my job.'

'Your job as a rap artist?'

'Of course, my job as a rap artist. By the way, how's that great idea of yours going?'

I did nothing but smile and went on my way towards the health food bar. I wasn't going to tell anyone except for Chippy McGrath about my idea. Not yet anyway.

22

Lucy had been angry when she found out I'd visited her father. She said I'd hated her when she was trying to reform me. 'We only got close to each other when I stopped trying to change you,' she said. When I told her I'd wanted to stop her stealing little things she told me she wasn't going to steal little things any more, but she had a surprise for me which would make us really close for ever.

When I said that'd be nice of her she said, 'It won't just be nice. It'll be amazing!' Then she told me not to worry her dad about anything to do with us any more. 'Dad's got enough on his plate, what with Mum and trying to explain why God doesn't seem to take much interest in all the terrible things that happen in the world. No need to bother him with our little problems, which aren't going to exist any more anyway.'

That was all she said about it at the time, but of course I should have realized that something was going on. It wasn't that Lucy changed towards me. Nothing like that at all. In fact she seemed nicer to me, what shall I call it, more loving than ever before. But she went around with a secret sort of smile on her face. So naturally, from time to time, I felt that something was going on, although I had no idea of quite what. I suppose everyone feels that, don't they, when their girlfriend looks unusually happy. I suppose it's a dangerous signal, one way or the other.

I noticed a bit of a change in Chippy too since

he became Leonard McGrath and chair of SCRAP. He also treated me to a lot of his twisted little smiles, as though he was busy with something I probably wouldn't understand and which was, anyway, far too important for me to know about.

Of course I still did jobs for him and when I called round to the maisonette there were the people I'd got used to working with—Screwtop Parkinson, the getaway driver, and Ozzy Desmond, the burglar alarm man, all the old lot who'd known Chippy, as I had, long before he came out as Leonard. But when I went to Connaught Square, they all seemed to stop talking when I went into a room and I had the feeling they had plans I wasn't meant to know about.

I told Lucy how I felt Chippy had changed. It was one Sunday morning and she was in bed beside me with all her clothes off, staring at the ceiling.

'I think he's rather wonderful,' she told me.

'What, pretending to be all law-abiding and reforming criminals when he's running a whole bloody organization of cons!'

'That's brilliant! He's got Gwenny and all that lot at SCRAP completely confused. He's so daring! Like one of us.'

'Daring? Is that what he is?'

'Of course. And if you didn't know that, you'll soon find out.'

Funny thing was that with all this feeling of things going on that I didn't know about, and people not telling me, I began to feel more at home with Mr Markby on my regular calls to his office. Of course I had a few secrets from him, like the way I earned my living. I told him that I was

150

helping round a couple of restaurants in Notting Hill, where I'd found a flat. He seemed to be happy with that much explanation. Then he asked me how that friend of mine was doing, the one who'd fallen into the habit of stealing small articles of no great value.

'I think I've stopped her doing that,' I told him.

'You mean you made it clear to her where such behaviour can land her?'

'I think she got the message.'

'Well, congratulations!' There was a great delighted grin on my probation officer's face, as though he was a man in a betting shop who'd just won a four selection accumulator on the horses. 'You reformed her!'

'I did my best.' I tried to sound modest.

'Reforming people is a real talent!' The grin seemed to fall from Mr Markby's face and he looked troubled. 'I'm not sure I have the gift myself.'

He looked so sad that I felt I had to do my best to cheer him up. 'Oh, I'm sure you have,' I told him.

'So many people come through this office.' He was sounding really sad. 'They've just come out of prison and we're here to help them reform. And what do they do? Something calculated to send them back for even longer in prison. When I was young and enthusiastic I used to believe prison was like the National Health. You were meant to go in to it bad and come out better. But what would doctors feel like if everyone who came out of hospital felt they had to go back there immediately?'

'I suppose a bit depressed.' I felt really sorry

151

for him.

'Depressed is the right word for it.' Mr Markby was clearly in a mood to tell me all his troubles. 'I have a Jack Russell dog called Rosemary.'

'Female?' I wasn't clear how you could be both Jack and Rosemary, even if you were a dog.

'Of course. An intelligent dog. I suppose I mean bitch, in as many ways. But if a strange man appears in the house she has an irresistible urge to bite the ends of his trousers.'

I didn't know what to say, but I did my best to look sympathetic.

'I've tried everything I could think of to reform her. I've put her into her bed when she does it. I've given her extra biscuits on the rare occasions when she doesn't. But I really have to admit, I can't change her behaviour patterns.'

'I'm sorry,' was all I could think of to say.

'Thank you, but it's embarrassing. Sir Jonathan Peebles, Her Majesty's Inspector of Prisons, did us the honour of coming to a small dinner party my wife and I gave a week or so ago. I'd hardly given him a glass of sherry before Rosemary fixed her teeth in the ends of his trousers.'

'That was embarrassing?' It seemed to be the wrong way round, having Mr Markby making a full confession to me and expecting help and reassurance.

'Terribly embarrassing! They were fine trousers, I would say tailor-made. Savile Row. Scottish tweed, all that sort of thing. Rosemary obviously enjoyed getting her teeth into the ends of them. Sir Jonathan has perfect manners of course, but he was certainly irritated. He said something like, "Can't you call your bloody dog off?" I did my best of course, but I've simply failed to reform Rosemary.'

'I'm sorry.'

'And yet you've managed to reform this friend of yours.'

At first I didn't see the connection. Lucy didn't, so far as I knew, bite the ends of people's trousers. But then I said, 'I seem to have persuaded her.'

'Persuaded her? That's what you did.' He seemed to be thinking hard about it all and then he came out with, 'Perhaps that's because you've been a criminal yourself. It takes one to reform one.'

'Perhaps.'

'So should I do some sort of crime and then I might do my job better?'

I looked at Mr Markby and I was amazed, quite honestly. A tall, sandy-haired man I couldn't imagine climbing in through a kitchen window by night. He'd have been hopeless at it.

'No,' I told him. 'I don't think you should.'

'I was only joking.' It was the first time in all my dealings with Mr Markby that I'd known him to make a joke. He dropped the idea of taking to crime and quite suddenly he asked me how old I was. When I hesitated he said, 'I suppose you're over twenty-five?'

I admitted it.

'And I suppose you left school before A levels?'

I didn't know what this was all about but I told him I'd been self-educated in Wormwood Scrubs.

'So, A level passes wouldn't be necessary. Maybe a Diploma in Probation Studies instead. You know what I'm talking about?'

I had to tell him I had absolutely no idea.

'It's just something to keep in mind for the

future. We can discuss it when we meet again.'

But before we met again, something happened which changed everything.

23

My phone rang at the office and, after a small click which seemed to infect the telephones I used at work and at home, a voice said, 'Is that Miss Purefoy? My name is Henry Parkinson.'

'I'm Lucy Purefoy,' I told him. 'But who are you?'

'I go under the nickname of Screwtop. I've been instructed to meet you concerning the lady coming out of the bath.'

'Oh yes,' I said. 'I've been expecting a call.'

'We better have a meet. Shall we say 6.30 tomorrow in the Brummell Club?'

'Is that safe? My friend Terry goes there. I wouldn't want him to know.'

'He won't be there tomorrow evening. I can promise you that. He'll be out at another job. I'll be at the bar. Red hair, stocky build, sweet smile. You'll recognize me.' And he rang off.

As I put the phone down Julian at the next desk said, 'Who're you going to meet? Sounds as if you have a rather complicated love life.'

'You can say that again,' I told him.

In the days that followed, the fear and the excitement seemed to die away, and I remembered my date at the Brummell Club as though it was just another meeting with a client to discuss a campaign for an organic hair shampoo.

So I walked down Harrowby Street and passed the muscular chuckers-out with the feeling that I was going to just a routine meeting. But of course I couldn't go into that place without thinking about

Terry, and it was as if I was going back into a world I knew and where I felt at home, whereas I felt a sort of stranger in Robert's palace or at drinks with the Smith-Aldeneys. I was in a place of deep shadows with pools of light over the gambling tables and from the ceiling over one end of the bar. There I saw a small hunched-up figure with red hair and a cheerful smile. As I got nearer he straightened his back and said, 'You must be Lucy.'

I had to admit it. I had no choice in the matter.

'Sit down then. We don't want to shout about this, do we?'

I sat down on a high bar stool beside him. 'And you must be Screwtop,' I told him.

'The governor likes to call me that.' He smile died. 'But I can tell you my brain's 100 per cent when it comes to driving.' He fell into a resentful sort of silence and, as he gave no signs of buying me a drink, I got myself a glass of white wine and a Bacardi Breezer, which Screwtop finally told me was his 'usual poison'.

'The governor says you're to come along with us on the job.' He looked doubtful. 'We don't usually take them with us. Not amateurs.'

'I'm not exactly an amateur.'

'Why, you done jobs before?'

'One or two so far, yes.' I didn't tell him what Terry thought of my efforts at stealing. I was keen to get down to the details of my most ambitious project. 'Anyway, I know where the owner keeps what we're after.'

'So where are we going then?'

'It's called God's Acre Manor. It's near Aldershot.'

'How far out of London?'

'About an hour if there's no traffic.'

'There won't be much traffic at two in the morning.'

'Is that when we're going?'

'Take your average house. Everyone's asleep around three. Big family, is it?'

'Only one.'

'Single gent?'

'You got it!' I congratulated Screwtop. 'Oh, and a manservant, a sort of butler.'

'Sleeps in the house?'

'He drinks a lot of whisky. With any luck, he'll be out for the count.'

'Ground-floor kitchen, is there?'

'Yes, at the back of the house.'

'Sash windows?'

'I think so. It's an old manor house.'

'And you say you know where the gent keeps—whatever we're after?'

'Oh yes. I know exactly where he keeps it.'

'We'll take Ozzy Desmond along with us. He knows his burglar alarms and he can act as a peterman.'

'A what?'

'Specialist in opening safes.'

'It's not in a safe.'

'All the same, Ozzy'll be useful. He knows his silver so we might pick up all we can, if you don't mind.' Screwtop asking my permission was definitely sarcastic. All the same, I said I didn't mind.

'All right then.' Screwtop pulled out a Filofax and looked for a date in his diary. 'Next Friday, 21 July, if that suits you?'

'I'm sure it will.' I hadn't though it would be so

soon.

'Be in your car. What is it by the way?'

'A Polo. A bit beaten up, I'm afraid.'

'Don't worry. Always best to have an anonymous-looking motor. Be parked in the underground car park at Charing Cross. We'll pick you up there at two. Don't be late or anything.'

'I won't be.'

'Wear dark clothes. Jeans and a sweater. Trainers on your feet not to make a noise. Gloves. You got all that?'

'Oh yes, I've got it. I just wonder . . .'

'What do you wonder?'

'What I'm going to tell Terry about the night of the 21st, that's all. It's all come a bit soon.'

'You'll think of something, won't you? You're so clever.'

'I don't know about that. Will you have another drink?'

'Better not.' Screwtop suddenly felt the call of duty. 'Better report to the governor. I think we've covered everything.'

'Yes,' I told him. 'I think we did.'

Then he was gone and I was alone in the Beau Brummell Club finishing a glass of white wine. I was aware of a figure leaving the shadows further down the bar and moving to sit next to me.

'Ishmael!' I said. 'Is Deirdre with you?'

'No. When I come to this place, I don't bring Deirdre. It's not her sort of thing at all.'

'No, I suppose it isn't.'

'You came here with a friend. I saw you.'

'Not a friend. It was business. My advertising business.'

'Yes, of course,' he said, 'that's what it must

158

have been. For a moment I thought I recognized him. Must be mistaken.'

'Sorry, Ishmael,' I told him, 'I've got to get back to Terry. I hope you understand.'

'Yes, of course. Of course, I understand.'

I'll say one thing for Deirdre's Ishmael. Although he seemed to bob up everywhere, he was perfectly polite.

*   *   *

I told Terry I was going to a hen party in Aldershot. I know it was a lie but I'd planned that he'd know the truth soon enough, a truth that was going to bring us closer together than ever. 'It might go on till quite late, so don't wait up for me.'

'I wasn't going to.' He didn't seem exactly pleased, but that was because he didn't know what I was really going to do. 'Who are these girls anyway?'

'Oh, just people I used to know. Some of them I went to school with.'

'And where's this party taking place?'

Oh, if only he knew, I thought, he wouldn't be cross-examining me as though he was some sort of police officer or magistrate or something. But I still wasn't going to tell him until it was all safely over. If he even got a hint, I knew he'd be trying to stop me. But he went on looking at me suspiciously and he said, 'You're not going to see that Robin Thirkell, are you?'

'Why do you ask me that?' His question had made me a bit nervous.

'You were all over him one time. Kissing, that's how I remember it. And you had that lucky escape

159

last time—or at least that's what you told me!'

'Well, I'm not going to see him, I hope. He'll hardly be invited to a hen night.' What I really meant was I hoped he didn't see me. Anyway, I was getting tired of all these sulky questions about what was intended to be just a great night for both of us. I said, 'You don't mind me going out with the girls, do you?'

'Of course not. You can come and go as you please.' But he didn't sound exactly sure about it.

'Well,' I said, 'thank you very much.' I pretended to be quite upset that he was questioning me about my movements. 'Just you wait,' was what I didn't say, 'until you see what I'm going to bring you back.' Instead I turned the questioning on him. 'So what are you doing this evening?' I asked.

'Staying in, I suppose.' He did seem a bit sulky. 'Perhaps read a book.'

'Really? What are you going to read?'

'Mr Markby gave me a book. All about the Probation Service. It's about reforming people.'

'You don't want to read that, do you?'

'I might have a look at it.'

'I won't be gone long. And then we'll have more interesting things to discuss than the Probation Service,' I promised him.

And then he smiled and said, 'I'll miss you,' which was all I needed to speed me on my way.

*   *   *

The difficulty was knowing how to fill in the evening. You see, I had to leave Terry at what might be a reasonable time to set off for a hen party in Aldershot and my actual date wasn't until

160

two o'clock in the morning. Well, we were going to meet up and leave London about two o'clock in the morning.

I went and sat in the darkness of a cinema, watching car chases and shootings in a film with a story which I had too much else to think about to understand.

When I came out, I tried to feel the excitement Terry had described to me, but all I could think of was the long light July evening, which seemed to stretch out like a lifetime before me. I parked near the Close-Up Club and took my suitcase from the boot of the Polo. In the lavatory, I changed from my wrap-around dress, suitable for a hen night, into the jeans, black sweater and trainers that Screwtop had recommended. There was no Deirdre or Ishmael, in fact no one in there I knew at all. I had ordered a plate of pasta and thought that crime was rather like the National Health Service. There was a great deal of hanging about attached to it. I almost gave it all up then, but I remembered that by the morning I would truly have understood Terry, I would know exactly what he felt and we would be together completely, absolutely and for always. I finished the bottle of Valpolicella that came with the spaghetti and drove to the underground car park.

There was nothing to do but go to sleep in the car. I'd turned on the radio and bits of news from all over the world, war, death, skulduggery and starvation, drifted into the Polo. I switched it off and, suddenly tired, wondered what I was doing, alone in an underground car park, until I fell asleep.

I was woken up by someone knocking on the

161

window. I turned my head and opened my eyes to see Screwtop's grinning face on the other side of the glass. I opened the window and felt the first tingle of excitement that would grow on me during the night.

24

I don't know why it was, but I couldn't quite credit the story about the hen party. I got a feeling that I didn't like at all that Lucy was lying to me. When we first met I wouldn't have given a single solitary fart about that, but now it seemed that I cared very much, perhaps too much, as it turned out, for my own good, or certainly the good of Lucy.

Why didn't I believe her? I suppose I'd seen so many of my friends and people I'd worked with telling lies in court. Made up stories about what they were doing on the night in question, faked alibis, any sort of 'pork pies', as Chippy used to call them in the days before he became Leonard. Anyway, they always told these lies with a sort of wide-eyed look of sincerity—the look Lucy gave me when she talked about the hen party in Aldershot. I mean, she'd never mentioned this lot of girl friends before. Yes, she'd mentioned her friend Deirdre, who she met for drinks at the Close-Up from time to time, but that was all.

Then I noticed that nearer the date she got, well, sort of excited. A lot of the time she seemed to be thinking of something else entirely and then she'd keep coming back to the subject, saying, 'You don't mind really, do you?' or 'I'm sure it's better for our relationship that I do things on my own from time to time.' What sort of things was she thinking of doing on her own? That was what I couldn't help wondering. I suppose you'll say I was unreasonably jealous, but just look at her previous. When we first met she had this boyfriend, Tom, who fizzled out but was no doubt somewhere still alive on the face of the earth. Then there was that Robin, who had his tongue halfway down her throat when I caught them kissing in the Intimate Bistro. I know he had tried his luck when she went for a dinner party in his big country house, and he had plenty of money. So was it another date with Robin that Lucy was getting so excited about?

I know what you're going to say. That I was well in love with Lucy by this time and that was perfectly true. It all seemed to be going well. I was sure I'd put her off the habit of stealing little things which didn't suit her at all. And life had never been better than it was in All Saints Road. I got used to cooking in the way I'd seen it done when I worked at the bistro. Lucy kept saying there was something needed to make us feel really close, but to be honest I felt close enough already. I'd have been quite happy to keep things going as they were. Which is why I got more than a little upset when she spun me what I suspected was a false alibi.

Then there was the business of the suitcase. It was the evening before the alleged hen night. I was cooking in the kitchen and I looked out of the window and saw her put her small suitcase in the boot of the Polo. There was something about the way she did it, looking to see there was no one watching, as though she had blagged her own suitcase or something. When I asked her about it she got quite angry. 'I told you I might have to stay the night with one of the girls,' she said. 'What's the matter? Do you want to search my luggage? What are you, some sort of customs officer?'

I tried to calm her down by telling her that of

course I didn't mind her going to meet her girl friends and we sort of made things up, though I was still not entirely convinced. Then the time came when she put on her new wrap-around dress and set off in the Polo and I was left alone in the flat, still not quite sure she'd told me everything.

I went to bed quite early but I couldn't sleep. Eventually it got to past two in the morning. I'd had a very restless few hours, thinking things over in my mind, imagining all kinds of stuff. I was still not sure of her, so I decided to ring her on her mobile. Perhaps, I thought, she'd still be up and partying with the girls.

Well, she must have pressed the green button to answer my call and I heard her voice and a man's voice calling something I couldn't quite hear. Then she cut me off and the line went dead. After that there was no point in trying to go to sleep.

25

The car which would become the getaway and was now the get-to-it was an anonymous Rover. I had been introduced to Ozzy Desmond, the peterman, the expert in getting into safes. Screwtop seemed a little in awe of Ozzy, who was, quite obviously, at the top of his profession. He was a tall, thin person with long, bony fingers who wound himself up in the seat next to the driver. He'd obviously decided neither to speak nor to look at me, as though I were a quite unnecessary complication in the job ahead, which, from his point of view, I suppose I was.

So I sat alone in the back of the car telling Screwtop, as we drove at speed but not, Screwtop assured me, 'getaway speed', the way I always went in my Polo out of London and towards my home. It was as we were crossing Clapham Common and Screwtop was asking me if I knew the house really well, a fact he seemed anxious to have confirmed, that my mobile rang in the pocket of my jeans. I pulled it out and must have pressed the green button as I answered Screwtop's question: 'Know God's Acre well?' 'Every inch of it,' I told him. Then I put the phone to my ear and heard Terry's voice as Screwtop almost shouted from the front of the car, 'Put that bloody thing away. Don't answer it.'

So I had to switch Terry off. Screwtop was right, of course, I couldn't speak to Terry then. It would all have to wait until we were together, more together than ever, when I was safely back in

Notting Hill Gate.

We'd sped, and I mean sped, round the M25 and turned off along the M3 and then I could see in the headlights the tall familiar trees round Folly Hill, where Terry and I had our picnic and made love for the first time. I leaned forward by the coiled-up Ozzy to give Screwtop careful directions.

Now I have to go into a bit of geography. Like all the smart houses in our neighbourhood, God's Acre had big gates between pillars topped by heraldic devices, in Robin's case a pair of curly tailed dragons. You had to press a number on one of the pillars for the gates to swing politely open and invite you in. The driveway could take you right round to the back of the house, to a sort of tradesman's entrance where it joined a narrow lane which led to a wider road, a roundabout and then the main road to Aldershot.

When we stopped in front of the main gates I dug my Filofax out of my bag and found the magic number. I got out of the car, pressed the numbers and the gates swung open in obedient silence. From that moment, it all seemed like a dream. An exciting dream of course, just as Terry had told me. I was where I shouldn't have been, doing something I shouldn't do, and, as the car crunched the gravel, I was listening for every sound, staring into the darkness for every danger, feeling more alone than I think I'd ever felt.

The gates swung to behind us and there came what seemed to me an ear-splitting chorus loud enough to wake the dead. The dogs were barking in the stables at the side of the house. Screwtop wound down the car window, calling at them and shouting, 'Fucking dogs, we should give them a whiff of something!' With my new self-confidence and general feeling of being team leader, I promised to deal with it. Screwtop was going to take the car to the back of the house and find the kitchen window and I'd join them there after I'd dealt with the dogs.

The stable door wasn't locked and I saw the bright eyes of four dogs glowing in the shadows. I suppose they could smell someone they knew and so the loud barks turned to low grumbling whimpers. I found sleek heads to pat and called them softly by their names, 'Judy' and 'Marlene', 'Greta' and 'Virginia'. They obviously liked to hear their famous names as they licked my hands and then composed themselves for another long sleep. I felt I'd been a huge success with the dogs and after that nothing else was going to be a problem.

The dogs would wake up Max and he'd be a match for any burglar, Robin had told me. Even when he said it, I rather doubted it. Max's intake of whisky was such that I felt sure the short chorus of barks wouldn't have disturbed his sleep in his rooms over the garage. When I got to the back of the house where the car was parked that seemed to be right. My mates (that's what I called them to myself) had cut a pane of glass out of the kitchen window, Screwtop had put his hand through and, as I came round the corner to join them, Ozzy Desmond had inserted himself into the open window and was oozing, like some long and dark-suited snake, over the window sill and across the kitchen sink.

Screwtop, who had become decidedly friendly since I silenced the dogs, helped me in through the window and he squirmed across the sink after me.

And then we were in the house with our torches switched on, unheard, unknown and unwelcome visitors, and I felt the extraordinary excitement Terry had described. We were taking the great risk for the great prize and I felt almost like laughing at the danger. Now I knew exactly what Terry felt. We were companions in crime, I suppose you might call us that, and from now on Terry would have no secrets from me.

As we moved, how quietly we moved, from room to room our torches picked out familiar objects, a cherub on a marble column, photographs on the piano of Robin as a boy, an empty champagne bottle on an inlaid table. In the dining room there were the remains of a solitary meal, not yet cleared away by Max. As Ozzy Desmond finished removing the silver from the sideboard I whispered to Screwtop, 'Shall I go and get it now?'

'You want a bit of help?' the whisper came back.

'No, thanks. I can manage it perfectly well on my own.' Once again you can see how confident I was. No one knew I was there. I felt invisible. I could manage anything.

I remember going up the staircase in the old days, probably a bit drunk, laughing at one of Robin's ridiculous bits of gossip. Not now. Not any more. But all that was long ago. In the days before I met Terry and my life seemed to change. I felt elated but not guilty. We really weren't taking anything Robin couldn't afford to lose.

As I reached the bedroom door I switched off my torch and put it in my pocket. I stood in the pitch dark, gripping the cold china door handle.

Of course I knew how Robin slept. It was a deep

sleep and it was hard to wake him, but during it he would make odd murmuring noises with an occasional meaningless word thrown in, as though he was still gossiping in his dreams.

It was so dark that I had to feel along the wall until I got to the picture frame and, as I touched it, some dark cloud must have moved in a gusting wind and faint moonlight crept across the room. I could see the tall posts of Robin's bed with their leaves on the top and even made out the naked woman engrossed in drying herself after her bath. She came off the wall with no trouble at all. As Robin muttered something incomprehensible I was out of his room, having closed the door as carefully as I could. I was halfway down the dark passage with £400,000 worth of Pierre Bonnard swinging at my side.

As I carried the picture down the dark passage, I heard a car driving away fast. Then I started down the stairs and suddenly found myself walking into the brilliant light of Robin's great candelabra. I realized there were people in the hall. I heard voices but for some reason I didn't turn back. And at the bottom of the stairs, much to my amazement, I saw Ishmael step forward as if to greet me.

'Ishmael,' I greeted him, but he wasn't smiling.

'Detective Sergeant Ishmael Macdonald.'

He was a rap artist. I felt sure he must be joking until he said, 'Are you Lucy Agnes Purefoy?'

'You know I am,' I told him. 'But I can't think where you heard about the Agnes.' (As a matter of fact it was my grandmother's name, but no one ever used it, certainly not me.)

'I'm arresting you for suspected burglary.'

As he said this one of the policemen took the Bonnard and I looked up the stairs to see Robin in a silk dressing gown staring down at me. Ishmael was reciting some rigmarole about anything I said being used as evidence against me at my trial, but I wasn't listening. It all seemed part of the dream and I still hoped that I would wake up in bed with Terry. But then I felt something like a cold clutch on my wrist and I looked down and saw that Ishmael and I were joined by a single handcuff. This had to be a dream I decided. 'But you're a rap singer,' I told him.

'Only as a hobby.' He was actually smiling. 'At work I'm DS Ishmael Macdonald, one of the Met's few Caribbean detective sergeants. Shall we go out to the car?'

'Deirdre never told me.' I don't know why I said that.

'No, I think she finds it rather embarrassing.'

As I went out of the front door I passed Max wearing pyjama trousers and a none too clean vest. At last, when we got out into the driveway, the dogs started howling. I think it was then I woke up. The dream was over.

26

As I said, I hadn't slept after I tried to ring Lucy and she cut me off. After that I lay awake for what seemed a long time, thinking the worst things about her and really surprised at how much I minded. I thought about leaving her perhaps, but then decided that life wouldn't be much good without her. Only I was going to be quite firm with her and insist that she didn't go on with some ridiculous story about an all-girls party. I wanted to know the truth, and at about 3.30 in the morning the telephone rang by the bed and I found it out.

'Hello.' It was Lucy's voice. 'Sorry to wake you up.'

'I wasn't asleep. Where the hell are you?'

'Hell's rather a good word for it. I'm in Aldershot Police Station.'

'What are you doing there?'

'Just about to be taken down to my cell. This is the one telephone call I'm allowed.'

'What is it? Were you drunk driving?' It was my first thought because she had had quite a bit to drink when she drove back from Robin Thirkell's place that time previously. I didn't approve, and I told her so.

'Not exactly.'

'Then what?'

'Something I thought you'd understand.'

'What would I understand?'

'Burglary. Isn't it your special subject?' She stopped talking then and I heard some male voices in the background. Then she said, 'I shouldn't say any more about it now. They're going to interview me later. After my sleep in the cell.'

'I can't believe it!'

'Why not? You know what it's like, don't you?'

'But what do they say you took?'

'I can't explain it all now. I did it all for you, Terry. Oh, by the way, the Polo's still in the Charing Cross underground car park. I'll give the key to these policemen here. I've got to go now.'

'All right, but . . .'

'I'm going to miss you, Terry. That's all I know. I'm going to miss you.'

And then the line went dead. I got up, made tea and smoked until it was morning and I could do something about getting a brief for Lucy. I didn't want to ask Chippy, as all the briefs he'd recommended to me during our long association had seemed to work hard to get me guilty verdicts. In the end, I rang my probation officer, Mr Markby. I told him that my friend who I'd tried to stop thieving was now in serious trouble, in fact she'd been arrested for burglary.

'Then you'd better tell me who she is.'

'Lucy Purefoy.' I couldn't hide her any longer. Anyway, she'd soon be in all the papers. 'I met her through SCRAP.'

'Lucy Purefoy, yes! That's the trouble with these girls from SCRAP. They start off falling in love with the criminal and end up falling in love with crime.'

In the end, he recommended a guy called Peter Bethell, who was on some committee with SCRAP. He managed to persuade Mr Bethell to get himself down to Aldershot by the time Lucy got interviewed. I've kept the official note of that interview, like I kept everything to do with Lucy, to have something to remember her by. I don't suppose her answers did her a whole lot of good at the time.

INTERVIEW CONDUCTED WITH LUCY AGNES PUREFOY AT 10.30 A.M. ON 22 JULY 2005 BY DS ISHMAEL MACDONALD IN THE PRESENCE OF DC GUTTERIDGE. PUREFOY HAVING CHOSEN TO BE LEGALLY REPRESENTED, THERE WAS ALSO PRESENT MR PETER BETHELL OF THE FIRM BETHELL, SHERMAN AND PENSOTTI.

DS MACDONALD: I am Detective Sergeant Ishmael Macdonald and this is Detective Constable Gutteridge, who is taking a full note of this interview. You are Lucinda Agnes Purefoy?

PUREFOY: You know perfectly well who I am.

DS MACDONALD: This is for the record.

PUREFOY: All right. And for the record you're Ishmael, described as a rap artist, friend of my friend Deirdre, who you met through SCRAP.

DS MACDONALD: You shouldn't be asking me questions.

PUREFOY: If you want me to answer your questions, you must answer mine.

DS MACDONALD: Very well. I met Deirdre through SCRAP when I came to speak there as a sergeant, representing the police.

PUREFOY: They made you a detective sergeant?

DS MACDONALD: Certainly.

PUREFOY: How many detective sergeants from

174

the Caribbean are there?

DS MACDONALD: The Metropolitan Police is no longer a racist institution. I am one of the many detective sergeants of different ethnic origins.

PUREFOY: Many?

DS MACDONALD: Some. DC Gutteridge, will you leave this part of the interview out of the record?

DC GUTTERIDGE: Not possible. It's my duty to record the whole interview verbatim.

DS MACDONALD: Oh, very well. (To Purefoy) Would you like a cup of tea?

PUREFOY: No thanks. Your tea's disgusting. You could stand a spoon up in it. If you had an Earl Grey tea bag you could just wave it over the water.

DS MACDONALD: Well, we haven't. Now, you were found leaving God's Acre Manor at 3.00 a.m. in possession of a valuable painting.

PUREFOY: What I want to know is how you got there.

DS MACDONALD: I have to suggest it was because of what you told me.

PUREFOY: What I told you when?

DS MACDONALD: I have warned you. It's not for you to ask the questions.

MR BETHELL (SOLICITOR): I think my client is entitled to know what you suggest she said and on what occasion.

DS MACDONALD: Oh, very well then. It was in the Close-Up Club and you said you had a great idea that would bring you closer to Terry Keegan, a man with a lengthy criminal record. It seemed possible that you were planning to participate in some crime to please your lover.

So you were kept under observation.

PUREFOY: Is that why you kept bobbing up wherever I went? And were my telephone calls getting interfered with?

DS MACDONALD: Once again, I must warn you not to ask me questions.

PUREFOY: I thought you were a rap artist. I've heard you rap.

DS MACDONALD: Rap is my spare-time hobby. Serving with the Metropolitan Police is my full-time calling. Will you please answer my question now? How did you get to God's Acre Manor last night?

PUREFOY: I'll leave you to find that out.

DS MACDONALD: As we approached the house, a car drove rapidly away from the back entrance. Did you come in that car?

PUREFOY: If you heard that why didn't you drive after it and find out?

DS MACDONALD: At that stage we couldn't drive through the main gates.

PUREFOY: You mean because you hadn't got the secret number?

AT 10.45 A.M. MR BETHELL ASKED TO BE ALLOWED TO GIVE SOME ADVICE TO HIS CLIENT. THERE WAS A SHORT DISCUSSION BETWEEN THEM AT THE OTHER END OF THE ROOM. INTERVIEW RESUMED AT 11.00 A.M.

PUREFOY: I'm sorry. I'm told I shouldn't have said that. I mean about you being a good rap artist.

DS MACDONALD: As I have clearly said, it would

be better if you confined yourself to answering my questions. Did you enter the house through the kitchen window?

PUREFOY: That's for you to find out.

DS MACDONALD: We found no fingerprints. Did you and your companions wear gloves?

PUREFOY: I didn't say I had any companions.

DS MACDONALD: We found foot marks. There must have been at least three of you.

PUREFOY: Must there?

DS MACDONALD: You were seen lately in the company of a man called Parkinson, sometimes known as Screwtop.

PUREFOY: You mean you saw him in the Brummell Club.

DS MACDONALD: How did you know that man?

PUREFOY: I think he once knew Terry.

DS MACDONALD: What were you talking about when you were with him in the Brummell Club?

PUREFOY: I think we discussed the weather. Oh, and American foreign policy.

DS MACDONALD: Was he with you when you stole the picture?

PUREFOY: I've told you, I was alone. There was no one else with me. No one.

DS MACDONALD: Then who was driving away in the car? Was it perhaps your lover, Terry Keegan?

PUREFOY: No, it certainly wasn't.

DS MACDONALD: You see? You are capable of answering a question. Who was it then?

PUREFOY: I don't know. I have no idea. Please don't go on asking me to do your detective work for you.

DS MACDONALD: Would you like a cup of tea?

PUREFOY: I've told you. I'd hate a cup of your tea and I don't want to answer any more questions. I want to go to sleep.

DS MACDONALD: We'll see how you feel about it later.

PUREFOY: I still won't want to answer any questions. Oh, by the way, give my love to Deirdre. But tell her she might have warned me you were a sneaky member of the Metropolitan Police.

THE INTERVIEW ENDED AT 11.25 A.M.

27

After the interview I stretched out on the bed in my police cell and went back to sleep. Sleep seemed to be the only way of getting through the next days, weeks, maybe years of my life. I'd done all I wanted to do in the interview. I realized it wasn't exactly what I ought to have done and that I was a bit rude to the alleged rap artist cop in disguise, but I couldn't help that. I was more sorry that I had to disappoint Mr Bethell.

Peter Bethell, he explained when he turned up rather to my surprise at the police station, was a 'close personal friend' of Orlando Wathen, the previous chair of SCRAP who was so puzzled by the causes of crime. I quickly discovered that the two shared a house together, so the relationship was altogether close and permanent.

Mr Bethell looked like a middle-aged schoolboy. He had a lock of brown hair, hardly tinged with grey, which fell untidily over his forehead. He had a ready grin which varied between the ingratiating and the cheeky. He spoke rather fast, sometimes as though the general excitement of entering prison and talking to criminals was almost too much for him. He was, as I was to discover, a sort of criminal's groupie. He spoke of the well-known felons he had defended, figures like Oscar Snell, the murderer who buried two extra bodies in a graveyard, and Rory Baxter, the Bond Street bank robber, as though they were great stars of the stage and screen and he was their producer, or at least their agent. He was obviously delighted to meet me and thought he might also be able to turn me into a star. I'm afraid he was impressed by the fact that my dad is a bishop.

'Of course it was a joke,' he told me when we first met.

'What was a joke?'

'You taking your friend's picture. Thirkell was your friend, wasn't he?'

'Once. Not recently.'

'Anyway, you took away his picture as a prank, meaning to give it back to him, didn't you?'

'No, it wasn't a prank. It was entirely serious.'

'What do you mean, it was serious?'

'It was a serious attempt to commit a serious crime. Unfortunately it turned out that I wasn't very good at it.'

'You're not telling me you did it to get a share of 400,000?'

'No, I'm not telling you that.'

'Then for what?'

'Because I wanted to really understand Terry. Because I wanted to feel what he felt. Because I wanted us to be really together. Because I love him. Oh, I know it sounds stupid.'

'Yes, it does.'

'I don't expect you to understand.'

'Please don't say any of that in the interview.'

'Why not? It's the truth.'

'Oh, good heavens!' He looked so boyish then that I felt sure he was going to come out with, 'Oh gosh!' but he went on, 'If everyone I defended felt they had to tell the truth in interviews we wouldn't get many of them off.'

'I can't help it. I just feel I've got to tell the truth and, what do they call it, the whole truth.'

'For the moment, let's keep your boyfriend, Terry, out of this. Where does he live?'

'Notting Hill Gate. We live together.'

'What's he do? I mean what's his job exactly?'

'Thief.'

Mr Bethell looked as though he had walked through an open door which had then banged shut and struck him smartly on the head. He seemed surprised and pained. 'Then for God's sake let's keep his name out of this,' is what he said.

'All right. I won't mention Terry.'

'I was talking to the detective sergeant . . .'

'The rap artist.'

'I don't know why you call him that.'

'Ask him. He'll know.'

'We won't bother about that. He says you came with two other people, who drove away.'

'I'm not going to answer any questions about them.'

'Were they thieves as well?'

'I'm not going to tell anyone about them.'

'Men of bad character, perhaps, who forced you to help them steal the picture?' Once again, as at the start of our conversation, Mr Bethell looked suddenly hopeful.

'It's just me that's responsible for all this. I'm not blaming anyone else.'

'The police would be grateful if you gave them some names.'

'I'm not naming names. Not for the rap artist or anyone. I'm not going to get anyone else into trouble.'

Mr Bethell's spirits sank. Once again he looked like a schoolboy who'd been told that he'll be off sweets at least for a week.

'When this interview's over,' he said, 'I'll have a word with your father, the bishop. I'm sure he'll have some sensible advice to give you.'

'Oh please,' I begged him, 'don't drag Dad into this. He's had quite enough to worry about, what with the way God's been behaving lately.'

It was then they called us for the interview and I was determined to irritate the rap artist at least as much as I'd managed to irritate poor Mr Bethell, who, after all, was only trying to help me out of a hopeless situation.

28

Her father told me she was coming up the next day in the Aldershot Magistrates' Court. He said the question of bail would be considered.

'I can't believe it,' he said. 'Is this something you planned to do together?'

'Absolutely not! I told you, I wanted to make her stop stealing.'

'Oh yes.' He seemed surprised at having to remember. 'I didn't take you entirely seriously. I should have done, I suppose.'

'You certainly should.'

'It's so difficult.' The bishop seemed lost in a world he couldn't understand any longer. 'God has sided with President Bush, my dear daughter has been arrested for stealing and you're at liberty.'

'For the moment, yes.'

'I just don't know how Lucy will cope with life in the cells. Luckily we sent her to boarding school, which may have given her some sort of training for it.'

'Let's hope she gets bail.'

'Oh yes. Let's hope profoundly and of course I shall do some solid knee work for it. Although,' now the bishop sounded doubtful, 'I'm not sure this God really appreciates being prayed to any more. The world seems to be full of unanswered prayers.'

'I'm sorry about that,' was all I could think of to say.

'Her solicitor rang me. He wants me to give evidence on the bail application. He says they won't be able to refuse a bishop. Would you agree, with your experience of courts?'

'My experience of courts is you never can tell what they're going to do.'

'Well yes.' He sounded disappointed. 'The solicitor says you arranged for him to see Lucy. Is that true?'

'Yes, through my probation officer, Mr Markby.'

'That was good of you. Very good.'

'It was nothing much. I care about her.'

I don't know if he heard because he didn't answer. He might have gone before I said it to do some of that knee work from which he didn't seem to expect any great results.

*   *   *

The Aldershot Magistrates' Court was crowded. I guessed there were a lot of journalists wanting to write 'Bishop's Daughter on Theft Charges'. I could feel their excitement at Lucy's troubles and I hated them for it. But what I wanted most of all was to see Lucy. There was a fat bloke wandering round with a list and I asked him if I could see Lucy Purefoy.

'Purefoy, Purefoy . . . bail application. We should get to it around twelve o'clock.'

'I just wanted to see her before then. Where should I go?'

'You want to see Purefoy?' A smiling character came up to me. I put him down as of Caribbean extraction. 'I'm Detective Sergeant Macdonald, officer in charge of the case. And you are . . . ?'

'Terry Keegan,' I told him.

'Of course.' The DS's smile broadened. 'I have

184

heard you spoken of frequently when my prisoner was in the company of my girlfriend, Deirdre. In fact I think I met you once. What an extremely small world this is after all!'

'Amazingly small.' I thought I'd better agree with him. 'So can I just pop down and see her in the cells or wherever she is?'

'No.' Our world may have been small but it was no longer friendly. 'I'm afraid you can't just "pop" down into the cells, as you call it. Prisoners here are not able to receive visitors.'

'Not even if they're friends of the officer in charge of the case?' I did my best to smile back at him.

'Particularly not if they are friends of the officer in charge of the case. In the Met we are taught to act without fear or favour.'

'I must see her though.'

'Of course you will see her.'

'Thank you.' It seemed the Old Bill had a bit of a heart after all.

'You will be able to see her from the public gallery. I advise you to go up there now to be sure of a place in the front row.'

So I sat in the public gallery and in time the magistrates came in. In the middle was Madam Chair, a large grey-haired woman with the look of someone who had just discovered that her dog has done a huge shit on the white carpet in the lounge. On one side of her was a burly-looking character with the physique of a nightclub bouncer who had something in his buttonhole, perhaps a trade union badge. Anyway, I told myself he was the sort that might take a fancy to Lucy and want to do the best for her.

185

I wasn't too hopeful about the bloke on the other side of Madam Chair. He was a hawk-faced person with rimless glasses who might have been an off-duty headmaster and looked at everyone who came up for a decision as though they had been caught having sex in the playground and bringing shame to the high reputation of Aldershot Comprehensive. The most active person in the court, however, was the little clerk who sat under Madam Chair and kept bobbing up to give her advice, which sometimes she seemed to take, though often she treated him as though he was the same dog that did the mess on the carpet and I fancied she muttered, 'Down, boy. Down!'

So I sat there and listened to people applying for various things, like having their careless-driving trials or their soliciting-on-the-streets-of-Aldershot cases postponed. I saw the bishop, Lucy's dad, sitting behind a brief who took his place in the solicitors' row. I guessed that man was Mr Bethell, who my probation officer recommended as likely to do his best for Lucy. On the other side there was a small bald-headed man who'd greeted all the court officials as though they were close personal friends. I was sure he was there from the Director of Public Prosecutions as, at last, he plumped himself down in front of DS Macdonald, the Old Bill representative who had sent me up to the public gallery.

'*R.* v. *Purefoy*. Bail application.' The clerk read it out from a bit of paper. 'Application for bail. Put up Purefoy.'

So they did. And there she was, Lucy in the dock, a position I'd been in more times than I'd had hot dinners. It didn't seem to affect her or have changed her at all. She had, as she always did, half a smile and a look which meant that she hoped they would like her, but deep down she didn't care whether they did or not.

There was a bit of droning on. The DPP man, who turned out to be called Mr Hastie, took a while to explain that the accused was charged with stealing a picture of enormous value. During this, Lucy looked round and even glanced up at the public gallery. She saw me and smiled, and I did my best to smile back. For a moment it seemed we were alone in the court and then Madam Chair told Lucy she could sit down, as though she was giving her a real treat. Lucy sat down obediently and didn't look back to me again.

Then her brief, Mr Bethell, got up on his hind legs and said he was applying for bail. He said it in a silky sort of a purring voice which I'm sure he thought would get the magistrates on his side, but I noticed that Madam Chair and her two supporters didn't seem to be all that impressed. He obviously expected a better reaction when he announced that he was going to call the Bishop of Aldershot to give evidence. As he said this there was certainly no round of applause or even a smile from the bench. Then the chat went on more or less like this, beginning with Mr Bethell asking Lucy's dad if he was the Right Reverend Robert Purefoy, Bishop of Aldershot.

'Yes, I am.'

I could see the newspaper people in court licking their pencils and turning to a new page in their notebooks to write their 'Bishop Gives Evidence for Arrested Daughter' stories. Mr Bethell asked, 'And you are the father of Lucinda

Purefoy, who is here in the dock?'

'Yes, I am. In fact we always call her Lucy. Everybody does.' He gave what he hoped was a winning smile at Madam Chair, but it was not returned.

'As we know, your daughter, Lucy, is of good character with no convictions.'

'Only one or two for going too fast in that Polo car of hers. Women drivers! Well, you know what they are.'

I suppose the bishop thought this might get a laugh from the bench. In which case he was wrong.

'But Lucy has no convictions for dishonesty. She has never been arrested before?'

'Certainly not! Indeed she has worked hard helping convicted criminals to reform and lead an honest life. She joined SCRAP as a praeceptor.'

'What is SCRAP exactly?'

'Social Carers, Reformers and Praeceptors.'

'Lucy worked for them?'

'For the best part of this year.'

'As a praeceptor?'

'Yes.'

'Which means—for the benefit of those of us in court who may not have had a classical education . . . ?'

'Being a guide, philosopher and friend to some young offender freshly out of prison.'

'And did Lucy get paid for such work?'

'Not at all. It was quite voluntary. Lucy has always wanted to do a bit of good in the world.'

I looked at Madam Chair. Her expression was unchanged. It was as though she thought that wanting to do some good in the world was the next worst thing to a criminal conviction.

'If the bench grants her bail,' Mr Bethell was asking, 'would Lucy come and live with her parents at the palace?'

'I imagine not.' The answer seemed to have disappointed Mr Bethell. 'I imagine she will continue to live in her flat in Notting Hill Gate.'

'Will she live there alone?'

'No. With her boyfriend.' The bishop turned to speak directly to Madam Chair and explain, 'They are in a stable relationship.'

Madam Chair looked as though she knew what a stable relationship meant and she didn't think much of it.

'But she can visit you and you'll be able to keep an eye on her?' Mr Bethell asked.

'Yes, of course! Lucy and Terry will always be welcome at the palace.'

'Thank you, Bishop Purefoy.' Mr Bethell sat down, looking like a man who has done as much as possible with some pretty ropy material.

But now the man from the Director of Public Prosecutions was on his feet and Madam Chair's 'You have some questions, Mr Hastie?' was warmer than anything she had handed out to Mr Bethell.

'Can you tell the bench this, Bishop.' Hastie began. 'When you say that your daughter is in a "stable relationship", does she live with this young man as his wife?'

'They're not married.' The bishop looked puzzled.

'No, but they are living together and having sexual intercourse?'

'Let us hope so. God gave us our bodies as a source of pleasure and delight.'

189

'So you approve of sex before marriage?'

'I can't see why anyone should fail to do so.'

'Some sections of the Church wouldn't agree with you.'

'Some sections of the Church have failed to move with the times.'

'Talking about moving with the times, is it true that you're in favour of gay marriages in church?'

'I really can't see why not.'

'Doesn't the Bible forbid homosexuality?'

In his answer, Lucy's dad asked a surprising question. 'Do you enjoy prawn cocktail, Mr Hastie?'

Of course, the clerk of the court jumped up to speak urgently to Madam Chair, who told the bishop that he wasn't there to ask questions and that the bench failed to see what a prawn cocktail had to do with a bail application.

'I'm quite prepared to answer the question.' Mr Hastie was showing how fair he could be even though he was there for the DPP. 'Yes, Bishop. I do enjoy a prawn cocktail.'

'Then let me remind you. It's true that the book of Leviticus says, "Though shalt not lie with mankind, as with womankind: it is abomination."'

'I thought it did.' Mr Hastie obviously felt he'd scored a hit.

'But it also says, "Whatsoever hath no fins nor scales in the waters, that shall be an abomination." Therefore no shellfish and, in particular, no prawn cocktail!'

'What's that meant to prove?' Hastie obviously felt he'd been outsmarted.

'It proves that we needn't take too much notice of those ancient bits of desert law.'

Madam Chair probably missed the point of all this because she was having another whisper with the clerk of the court, who then spoke out for her. 'The bench wishes you to get on with matters relevant to this bail application.'

'Then I'll raise a matter very relevant to this bail application.' Mr Hastie had been handed a bit of paper by the DS in charge of the case, who had turned out to be Lucy's friend Ishmael.

'Is the man she's living with, as husband and wife, called Terry Keegan?'

'He is. And he's here in the public gallery.'

Almost everyone except Lucy turned to look at me. The DPP's man handed his bit of paper in to the clerk of the court.

'That's a list of Keegan's convictions. All for theft.'

Madam Chair and her two sidekicks received the list gratefully. Clearly they found it far more interesting than bits of the Bible.

'So, Bishop, if your daughter is granted bail on this serious theft charge she will be living, as man and wife, with a convicted criminal. I suppose you'll tell this court that you thoroughly approve of that?'

'Of course,' the bishop plunged in happily. I just wished he could keep quiet and not be so bloody forgiving about everyone. 'Jesus Christ was a convicted criminal,' he told Mr Hastie.

'But this man Keegan is a thief.'

'And Jesus was crucified between two thieves. May I remind you of the gospel according to St Luke?'

'If you have to,' Mr Hastie sighed.

'One of the thieves said to Jesus, "Lord,

remember me when thou comest into thy kingdom," and Jesus said, "Today thou shalt be with me in Paradise."'

'Are you suggesting that Terry Keegan is going to heaven?' Mr Hastie asked, to which the bishop replied, 'I think he's got a better chance than most of us.'

'One more matter.' Mr Hastie seemed anxious to get away from my chance of heaven. 'Your daughter is accused of stealing a picture from God's Acre Manor. Did she know Mr Robin Thirkell, who owns the picture?'

'Oh yes, he's an old friend of Lucy's. They used to be very close.'

'Were they in a relationship, as you call it?'

'Oh yes. Of course.'

'So the suggestion here is that your daughter stole a valuable picture from a house she knew well and from a friend who trusted her.'

'I suppose he trusted her, yes.'

'And this court is being asked to grant bail so she can live with a thief.'

'A thief who may enter the Kingdom of Heaven.'

'Thank you, Bishop.' And Mr Hastie sat down. I suppose he thought he'd done a great job.

Mr Bethell made a short speech after that, promising not to quote the Bible and stressing the fact that Lucy had never been in trouble before. Then Madam Chair, who hadn't cracked a smile during the whole proceedings, announced that they'd retire. I told myself that there was still a small hope, but I didn't really believe it.

I don't know why they retired. Probably to have a coffee, or go to the loo, or tell each other what shocking opinions Lucy's dad had about sex and

192

never mind about the Bible. Anyway, they were back ten minutes later and for the first time there were smiles on the faces of Madam Chair and both the sidekicks.

'We have decided that we cannot grant bail in this case,' Madam Chair was delighted to say. 'The defendant will be remanded in custody. Take her down.'

Lucy stood up and was removed to the cells. She didn't turn to look at me but I was ready, however badly I felt, with smiles of encouragement.

As we left court I asked DS Ishmael Macdonald when I could get to see Lucy.

'You'll be able to visit her in Holloway,' he said.

Holloway. That wasn't particularly good news.

29

What I really couldn't bear about that so-called bail application was the way they treated my dad.

All right, I know Robert lives in a world of his own. All sorts of things seem important to him which have never seemed particularly important to me, although I'm sure we felt close to each other in the days when I wanted to do some sort of good in the world.

Since that time I know he's been worried about God, who seems to have got too close to people like Bush and Blair for Robert's liking. I know he doesn't think there's anything wrong with gay marriages and, quite honestly, I can't see what's so wicked about that. And he had some really interesting ideas about thieves getting into heaven which that awful woman up on the bench might have been well advised to listen to, instead of allowing Robert to be teased and baited and knocked all round the courtroom by that poncey little man from the Prosecution Service. Of course, I blame that Mr Bethell, who I don't think ever understood my case, but it must have been a horrible experience for Dad and I'm really sorry.

Those charming policemen in Aldershot had told me terrible things about Holloway, but to tell you the truth I didn't find it so bad as all that, not at least when you compared it with the horrible boarding school I went to in Ludlow. Robert and Sylvia sent me there because they thought I was an only child who'd be lonely at home, so they packed me off to St Swithin's, where I was a good deal more lonely, at any rate to start with. Looking back on it, I think I was made more welcome, and immediately got on better with the other girls, in prison.

I was in a dorm with four others (at Holloway, that is). We had to share one loo, which at times was difficult, but we could wear our own clothes and not those dreadful gym tunics they forced us into at St Swithin's. The food was equally stodgy, but at least in Holloway you got bacon and eggs for breakfast, which was an improvement on the awful St Swithin's soggy cornflakes. It's true that there were cockroaches in Holloway—you could watch them marching along the window sills—but it didn't have St Swithin's smell of over-boiled cabbage mixed with the drains. And as for the girls—well, I'll tell you more about them later.

The thing was that I was what they called a 'remand prisoner'. That's to say, I hadn't been tried and convicted, not yet. So I could have as many visits as I wanted. I had hardly looked around, let alone got used to the place, when Terry came to see me.

We sat at a table in the small, crowded visiting hall, with girls seeing their boyfriends or their children and some persistent offending old dears with their grandchildren. I hadn't seen Terry since he was looking down at me from the public gallery in that dreadful magistrates' court, and I looked away because I couldn't stand the idea that we were going to be separated and I didn't know if I'd be able to bear it.

When they told me I was going to have a visit I was really excited and I couldn't wait to see Terry. But now, as we sat at the table and he looked at

195

me, strangely silent, in fact not saying anything at all, I felt a space between us that was much wider than the table.

'Well, here's a funny situation!' I said, as brightly as I could manage.

'I can't see what's funny about it.'

'Well, I'm in prison and you aren't.'

'I don't know what's funny about that.'

'It's not how we started out.'

'No, it's certainly not.'

'But we've ended up more together than we ever were before.'

'I'm in Notting Hill Gate and you're in bloody Holloway. How can we be more together than we were before?'

'Because now we've done all the same things.'

'That's what you always say.' He gave a big sigh, heavier than I thought was necessary.

'But now it's true! I did a more important burglary. I planned it on my own. All right, I wasn't particularly good at it.'

'You can say that again.'

'And I landed up in prison. Like you did, Terry.'

'Are you saying that's a good thing?'

'I'm saying now I can understand you completely. And of course I felt it, just like you said.'

'Felt what?'

'The excitement. You said it was the greatest excitement in the world, being in a house when no one knew you were there. Taking the risk of Robin waking up. You said that was the best feeling in the world.'

'I might have said a lot of things.'

'You know you said that.' I was going to be

196

seriously disappointed if Terry tried to wriggle out of it.

'All right, I said it. But you didn't have to try it.'

'I didn't have to. I wanted to.'

'And now look where it's got you.'

'It's not so bad.'

'What?' He obviously didn't believe me.

'I said it's not too bad. You can get bacon and eggs for breakfast.'

'I could cook you that at home.'

'I know you could, darling.' I put my hand on his across the table. Things were going better. 'I'm going to miss you.'

'I'll miss you too.' Then he kissed me. I wasn't behind a screen or anything. All we gave each other was a kiss and then the visiting time was over. It was a moment to enjoy, because it wasn't much use thinking about the future.

*   *   *

As I say, I was in a dorm with four other girls and one lavatory. I call them girls because that's what we called ourselves, as though we were quite young and not really responsible for our actions— although the crimes we were in for were, I suppose, quite serious.

Anyway, some of the girls were there when I arrived and still there after I left. There was Devira, a serious Indian girl who wore glasses and talked in a clear, precise voice quite slowly as though everyone she talked to had only a moderate understanding of English. There was Martine, a sensible and cheerful girl who had done a burglary to pay for crack cocaine that her mother had started her off on around her fourteenth birthday. There was Daisy, who was pretty, blonde and so quiet that you couldn't believe she'd ever been part of a gang of street muggers. Then there was Rachel, a dark-haired girl whose conversation usually started off with phrases like, 'When I was in Mexico City' or 'I met this guy in Zanzibar', because she had gone round the world and stayed in some of the best hotels, all on stolen credit cards.

There had also been a girl called Louise, who was a professional 'carer'. That is, she cared for old or sick people, I suppose for wages from the National Health. No one, it seemed, had been quite clear what she was in for, but then someone discovered what had happened. Louise had found the old man she was caring for so irritating that she had smothered him with the cushion off his wheelchair, pressing it tight across his mouth and nose until he died. This was a crime which the other girls thought unforgivable and Louise was in constant danger of being smothered or worse by the harsh judges of the Holloway establishment. In fact Louise was in such danger for what she'd done as a carer that she had been removed to a security wing to protect her from the other girls and I suppose I took her place.

*   *   *

'I work in the laundry,' I told Terry on one of his visits. 'And then I work out in the gym. Rachel's wonderful on the trampoline. She does sort of somersaults.'

'And Martine? You told me about Martine.'

'Martine doesn't do it because she's pregnant!'

'I hope you're not.' Terry looked worried.

'No, I'm not.' I didn't tell him that I wouldn't have minded. I wouldn't have minded at all. Then he began questioning me.

'You told me how you felt when you got into Robin's house,' he said.

'Yes, I told you.'

'You got in through the kitchen window, didn't you?'

'Yes, that's how I got in.'

'You weren't alone, were you?'

'What do you mean, I wasn't alone?'

'Well, you had other people with you. Screwtop, for instance.'

'Who told you that?'

'Never mind who told me. I get to hear things around the place.'

'I'm not saying anything about anyone else,' I told him. 'I'm fully responsible.'

'Then you're mad!'

'Probably.' I had to admit it.

'Tell them that Screwtop and Ozzy Desmond led you into it.'

'That was what Mr Bethell wanted me to say, but I can't do it.'

'Screwtop and Ozzy Desmond work for Chippy. Did Chippy know all about it? Did you talk to him?'

'I'm not saying.'

'You've got to tell them that they led you into a life of crime.'

'That wouldn't be true. They didn't.'

'Who did then?'

'You!'

199

Well, it was true, so I had to say it. Terry went rather quiet, but he still kissed me before he left.

*   *   *

The last girl to be hanged in England was Ruth Ellis, executed in old Holloway. Of course, we all knew about her. Rachel had read a book on her and told us all about it.

Ruth was only twenty-eight when it happened—not all that much older than me. She'd been a waitress and a nightclub hostess and married a dentist called George Ellis, but they soon parted. During the war she had a child by a French-Canadian serviceman and now I can't remember exactly what happened to the child.

Anyway she fell in love with a glamorous young racing driver of twenty-seven. His name was David Blakely. They lived together but she saw other lovers. They quarrelled and he drank a lot. David tried to leave her from time to time and he refused to tell her when he was going out and who he was going with. She'd had an abortion and got insanely jealous. In the end, and when she found him outside the Magdala Tavern, a pub near Hampstead Heath, she shot him dead.

At her trial Ruth was asked what she'd intended to do when she found her lover. It was her chance to say, 'I only wanted to scare him' or 'I was so emotionally disturbed that I didn't know what I was doing' or 'I'd just recovered from losing my baby and I think I went mad for a moment'—all that sort of thing. But all she did was to tell the truth. 'I intended to kill him,' was what she said. I respected her for that.

They never reprieved her. They say the executioner, Pierpoint, gave up his job after that, but she was still, we sometimes felt, hanging around our jail. There was a cat, for instance, called Ruth Ellis who was always mewing pathetically. And when I came in from the garden in the dark, or when I went up a lonely, poorly lit passage, I sometimes thought I saw the flickering image of a blonde young woman holding a fully loaded Smith & Wesson revolver. And if I blinked she was gone.

*   *   *

'I thought I saw a ghost,' I told Terry on his next visit.

'Of course you didn't.'

'Yes, I know I didn't. I just thought I did. The ghost of Ruth Ellis.'

'She was a murderer.' Terry sounded deeply disapproving of the idea that I should be associating with a murderer, even in a ghostly form.

'She might have had some excuse for what she did.' I spoke out for Ruth.

'There's no excuses, not for murder,' Terry told me seriously.

'I suppose not,' I said. 'All the same, they were wrong to hang her.'

Terry didn't answer that one. He changed the subject.

'I've been reading some of your books,' he said.

'My books?'

'Yes. The books you used to pass your A levels with.'

'My school books? Yes, I kept some of them.'

'I never got any A levels at all.'

'It doesn't matter,' I told him. 'Once you get out into life no one seems to bother about A levels any more.'

'I was reading your Milton book, *Paradise Lost*. That's a good one.'

'I never really cared for it,' I had to admit.

'What's wrong with it then?' Terry seemed unexpectedly protective of Milton.

'No jokes. I liked Shakespeare better. There are jokes in Shakespeare. Were you honestly reading *Paradise Lost*?'

'Quite honestly.'

'But why?'

'Maybe I want to better myself.'

'I don't want you better, Terry. I want you exactly as you are,' I told him, but then they rang the bell and the visit was over.

*   *   *

'Life! They gave me life!'

I was working in the laundry with Devira, who ironed sheets with grim thoroughness and determination. She folded them so she was only doing a quarter of a sheet at a time, but then slammed down the iron and flattened the pile mercilessly. She finished a sheet long before I had got mine under control so she attacked that as well. When the sheets were ironed to her satisfaction we stood apart, held one end each with part of it tucked under our chins and then we approached each other, refolding it neatly as we moved steadily together.

202

'I read in the paper where it says, "Life should mean life." Well, it does. That's what it means exactly. My life is in here. What have I got when I get out—an old woman no one wants around the shop?'

In general, we didn't discuss the reasons for us being in Holloway, but Devira was different. I'd heard she talked about what she'd done quite freely and often, so I knew a little about what she was going to tell me.

'He was my husband, you know. A horrible man.'

One sheet was now thoroughly folded and we parted to either end of another.

'Igbal.'

'Your husband?'

'The husband they decided I had to marry. They sent for him all the way from Chandigarh. Travel expenses paid for by my father out of the profits of our corner shop in the Edgware Road area.'

'I know that area.' I remembered honking my horn for Terry outside the maisonette and us buying a picnic. 'Plenty of Middle Eastern shops.'

'Ours is not Arab. Sikh shopping.'

'Yes, of course.'

Another sheet was folded and we started another.

'I tell you, Igbal was a truly horrible man.'

'Why did you marry him then?'

'It was long ago decided by our families. I had no choice whatever in the matter. Igbal was a very sexual person. He couldn't keep his hands still because of it.'

'I'm sorry.' I smiled, trying to lighten her mood a little. 'Is that such a terrible thing?'

'It is when you're as bad as Igbal. He looked bad. He smelt bad. His temper was bad and he was bad at sexual relations. But he wanted them. Even in the shop. He wanted me to come behind the bead curtain and do it for him. Even when I was busy serving a customer.'

'I'm sorry.' That was all I could say.

'Don't be sorry. I was just explaining why I had to kill him.'

We'd folded all the sheets we'd ironed and Devira sat down on a stool while I pulled another lot out of a big pile on the floor.

'How did you manage it?' By this time I genuinely wanted to know.

'When he was asleep.'

'Yes, but how?'

'I set fire to him.' Devira said it with a heavy sigh, as though having to tell this part of the story had begun to bore her.

'Wasn't that very difficult?' I asked, with my arms full of unironed sheets.

To this, the quiet, calm Indian girl answered simply, 'Petrol.'

'Now, you two. This is work time, not a mothers' meeting.'

'Yes, Miss.' Devira stood up obediently and we went back to work.

The screw who had ticked us off was called Helen, known as Hell, Wickstead. She had a short haircut and a voice which could carry down the longest corridor. I didn't like her, although I had an uncomfortable feeling that she liked me.

30

All the time I had been talking to Mr Markby, and having discussions about my future if I managed to get a bit of further education into me, I still told him that I was simply helping out in a couple of restaurants round Notting Hill Gate.

This wasn't entirely true. I was still working for Chippy, no longer doing the important jobs but some of the routine house-breakings he left to less important members of his group. Why was I still doing it? Because crime had been a way of life to me since I was a kid and there didn't seem to be another way to make sure of a reasonable income. I don't say I didn't feel bad about going on with crime when Mr Markby was doing so much to help me, because I did. But once I was away from his office and went to get instructions from some of his staff round the maisonette or the Beau Brummell Club, I could forget Mr Markby, or at least put him to the back of my mind and promise myself to attend to him later.

I was no longer part of the 'A' team and I was kept well away from Screwtop and Ozzy Desmond, I suppose because of my connection with Lucy. They were always afraid she was going to tell the police about them. They needn't have worried, because Lucy may have slipped into dishonest ways but grassing was not one of them. In fact she kept to the code of ordinary decent criminals as though it was something she'd been brought up to since her school days.

So I was sent out with what was definitely a 'B'

outfit, with Romeo Robinson and Alfie Barnet, who could be relied on provided they weren't asked to do anything unexpected and the instructions were brilliantly clear. What led Mrs Robinson to call her child Romeo I can't imagine. I suppose some African mums living round the East End of London have romantic ideas about their children, but this Romeo looked less like a heart-throb than a lightweight boxer grown old before his time. He'd been put into a number of fights to entertain the paying customers when he was younger and his nose had been well broken and his ears well cauliflowered before he gave it all up for the safety of life as a thief.

Alfie had probably, like me, never followed any entirely honest occupation. He was small, cheerful, able to squeeze through small windows and climb drainpipes. He could deal with simple burglar alarms and locks. Faced with anything more complicated, he would shrug his shoulders and grin as though it had all been a big joke anyway.

They weren't highly qualified for what seemed like a routine job. It was a house on the edge of Hampstead Heath. Romeo had been keeping observation and listening to neighbours and he was sure the family were away on holiday. The back door could probably have been forced by an intelligent child with a penknife, but Alfie seemed to expect a round of applause when he managed it. The burglar alarm was also no problem. So we made a routine entrance in search of such routine articles as silver, television sets, money and other possibly valuable pieces.

I told the others I'd take the bedrooms and walked up the main staircase. Oddly, there was a light on in the corridor and I remember wondering vaguely why. But the main thing for me was that the feeling I'd described to Lucy, the excitement of being in someone's house wondering if you were going to get caught, had gone completely. Quite honestly, if I felt anything at all it was boredom. I was sick and tired of the whole business. And then I heard the soft sound of music coming from an open doorway.

It seemed that I was past caring what happened, because I went to the doorway and looked. There was enough moonlight for me to see an old man with wispy grey hair fast asleep. The radio at his bedside was still playing long after he'd fallen asleep. Of course I could have gone in and nicked the radio, but you know what I did? You won't believe this, and I hardly believed it of myself. I went in and switched the radio off for him.

Then I went down the stairs and out of the front door while the others were still at work in the dining room. I was away across Hampstead Heath, away from the crime I didn't want to commit, and then I was back in Notting Hill Gate, still amazed at the change that had come over me.

Most of all I was looking forward to telling Lucy about it.

31

Terry came as early as possible that next visiting day. He seemed full of himself and very excited and said he had something important to tell me. When I asked him what, he said, with a sort of worried face I thought he'd put on for the occasion, 'I've been thinking.'

'Thinking about what?' I always feel a certain amount of dread when people say they've been thinking.

'Since you told me that I'd introduced you to crime.'

'Well, you did.'

'And of course I feel bad about it.'

'You needn't. It was quite exciting while it lasted. And Robin deserved to lose that picture anyway.'

He looked a bit nervous, as though he had a confession to make.

'I told Mr Markby I felt bad.'

'Do you tell Mr Markby everything?'

'Most things, yes. So I told him I felt badly.'

'Well, you needn't.'

'And now I'm going to tell him the big thing. But I'm telling you first.'

'What big thing is that?'

It was then he began to tell me a long story about being in a Hampstead house at night and turning off a radio beside an old man sleeping and then leaving suddenly. Just clearing off home.

'Why did you do that?'

'Because I was bored with it.'

'Bored with what?'

'Crime. And then I made the big decision.'

'What decision was that exactly?'

'Just to get out of it. Once and for all.'

He looked at me with what I thought was a superior sort of smirk, as though he'd moved into a higher, better world and left me far below him in Holloway Prison.

'Oh, that's fine, isn't it?' I said. 'That's just great! I get into all this to understand you. To bond with you. To feel like you. So we could be together. So now you're giving it all up, are you, to become Mr Markby's favourite good boy, and leaving me in this dump!' Well, it was what I felt and I had to say it.

'I don't want to leave you,' Terry said. 'I want to be with you. Always.'

'We'll have to see about that.' I got up. 'I'd better get back to the girls. They'll be needing help with the laundry.'

So I left him looking completely surprised and ten minutes before the visiting time was over.

Later that day, I was in Recreation with Martine, watching television. I suppose I must have looked a bit down in the mouth because she asked me what the trouble was. I told her, 'I've just fallen out with my boyfriend.'

'It's difficult to keep things like that going when you're inside,' she said. 'That's why a lot of the girls here are "prison bent".'

'What's that mean exactly?'

'They're heterosexual with their boyfriends when they're out. But like when they're in here they, well, do it with each other. Have you ever thought of that?'

I promised her, as we watched *Big Brother*, that I'd keep it in mind.

32

It was clear that Lucy and me had drifted apart and, quite honestly, I couldn't work out the reason why.

If anyone was to blame for our troubles I should have said she was, for taking part in a burglary which, of course, was a complete cock-up. From what she told me, and from what I heard around about Screwtop being connected with the job, it was pretty obvious that Detective Sergeant Ishmael Macdonald was on the case from the start. So what Lucy did was to walk straight into the arms of the law. But when I visited I couldn't blame her for it. I was very careful not to lay any blame at all. That's not what you want to hear when you're behind bars, believe me.

But what was it all for, for God's sake? During an earlier visit Lucy had told me what she took was a picture of a naked woman drying herself after a bath, which Robin Thirkell kept in his bedroom. What he kept it in there for I don't know, unless perhaps he got his rocks off looking at it, which I wouldn't put past the type of person he undoubtedly is. But was the amount of trouble she'd got into worth it? When I said that, she told me that I really didn't understand anything about her. She was probably right.

I had looked into her Milton book, which seemed to be written in a foreign language at first, but I began to read it with the help of the notes Lucy had written out. So I got to read about the old devil who turned himself into a snake to tempt the first woman to steal. I think the first woman must have been a bit like Lucy, she was so easily tempted to steal an apple which must have had even less value than the picture of the bint just out of the bath.

I was, quite frankly, gobsmacked when I told Lucy this and, far from being impressed, she brought my visit to an abrupt end. I mean, this was exactly what she had wanted to happen on the day she met me coming out of the Scrubs and she took me for a giant burger. Admittedly I wasn't all that proud of the way I carried on, but she worked hard on my case.

But now all that work had paid off and all she seemed to be was angry with me and disappointed. She seemed to be happier with the women she lived with in Holloway—them that set fire to sleeping husbands and all that sort of thing. When we discussed that Lucy's case might not be heard for around six months, at the start of the next year, Mr Bethell said he'd apply to a judge this time for bail, but Lucy didn't want it. She said her friend Martine was due to have her baby at any moment and she didn't want to leave her.

Whatever she thought about it or me, I was going to do my best to help Lucy. I couldn't believe she planned a job like that by herself. She must have been forced into it, or tricked into it, by the old firm I used to work for, or, come to think of it, I'd been working for ever since I first met Chippy McGrath all those years ago.

I thought I should be a bit more sure of my ground before I accused Chippy. Then I remembered that a picture was the cause of all the trouble. I had the number of all Chippy's

212

associates, so I rang his art expert, a bit of an old fart called Hughie Whitcombe. I got an invitation to a drink with Hughie at his club in Pall Mall. To get in there I had to look respectable and remember to wear a tie.

The Gainsborough was nothing like the old Brummell Club or even the Close-Up, where I'd sometimes been with Lucy. The Gainsborough seemed to be a place mainly used for sleeping. The old bald-headed porter was asleep behind his desk in the marble-tiled entrance hall. He thought Hughie was in there somewhere, but having been asleep he couldn't be quite sure where he'd got to. He led me across the hall and we had a peep through the half-open door of the 'smoking room', but there was no sign of Hughie there. Finally we discovered him wide awake alone at the bar, where the bloke in charge was leaning back against the shelf of bottles, his arms crossed, one hand clutching a dishcloth and his eyes closed. The few members at the tables talked quietly, afraid of waking this person up. Only Hughie sat with his eyes wide open, a grey-haired man whose glasses were continually slipping down his nose, wearing a tweed suit that looked as if it had lived with him for a long time and a spotted bow tie.

'You'd like a drink,' he welcomed me. 'Guests can't pay but I know you lot are always stuffed with folding money. Slip me a bit of it and we'll do our best to wake up Clive.'

I slipped him a tenner in a way which he didn't seem to mind the other members noticing. He then called 'Clive!' loudly so that the barman opened his eyes, looked startled and delivered a couple of whiskies quite quickly.

213

'Thank you.' Hughie gulped his and then asked me, 'How is Leonardo de Medici?'

'I don't know him.'

'No, of course you don't. I'm sorry. I always think of our friend Leonard as like the great Medicis of Florence. A brigand, of course, but deeply interested in art.'

The words came tumbling out of Hughie, high-pitched and quite excited. I knew he'd written for one of the posh papers and then been sacked, to be replaced by some girl he always said 'thought art was all about people videoing their own bottoms'. He'd got involved in the stolen picture business, first of all as a go-between, agreeing ransoms for stolen stuff, and then as Chippy's adviser on what was worth stealing or how to turn stolen art into money.

'Did Chippy ever say anything to you . . .'

'You mean Leonardo?' he corrected me. 'Let's show the greatest respect for an important patron of the arts.'

'All right, Leonardo.'

'Leonardo de Medici.'

'If you want. Did he say anything about a picture of a woman drying herself after a bath?'

'Oh! You mean the little Bonnard.'

'Is that what I mean?'

'Pierre Bonnard. Leonardo was going to "find" one for us. Picture of the painter's wife, Marthe, having got out of the bath. As Leonardo said, it would have been worth more if she'd been in the bath, but all the same it would have been a nice little earner.'

'Chippy . . . sorry, Leonard said he was going to get this picture?'

214

'It was going to come to us through the system.'

'But it never came?'

'I suppose there must have been some hitch.'

'Yes, I suppose there must.'

I didn't tell him that the hitch was that the thief in question had landed up in Holloway Prison. Hughie woke Clive the barman up and ordered more drinks. Then he said, 'Do stay for lunch if you can. It's very reasonable here, and if you'd like to contribute a little of your folding money . . .'

*   *   *

'You've done it all my bloody life. We did all the stealing for you and then we did the prison for you. All for you, you jammy bastard. We did the prison while you sat in that fucking maisonette and got richer and more respectable, and we all worked for you so you could become "Leonardo"—that's what Hughie calls you. The great soon to be Sir Leonard who does good work for poor misguided prisoners. You just used me. All my life. But this time you went too fucking far. You used Lucy to do your stealing and now she's in prison because of you, Chippy.'

I had caught him at work in SCRAP and, in spite of the protests of a worried-looking woman in the main office, when I got to him I didn't, as you can see, mince my words. I gave it to him absolutely straight.

'Don't ever use that word in here.'

'What word is that?'

'Chippy!' He scarcely whispered it.

'Chippy!' I said quite loudly. 'I'm going to use it. And I'll make sure Lucy uses it in court. She'll

215

have to explain why she went out stealing to get a picture for you. You organized the entire fucking job.'

'She volunteered. She made sure I'd help her do it. She threatened to make trouble if I didn't lay on a team for her.'

'Screwtop and Ozzy. That was the team, wasn't it?'

'Perhaps.'

'No perhaps about it. And Hughie was going to get the money for it.'

'I meant her to have her share.'

'Well, you'll get your share, Chippy. She's going to tell them the whole story in court.'

Chippy was sitting at his desk. He looked hunched-up, smaller than usual. He stared up at me, pleading.

'What can I do about it?'

'I don't know. Give her some sort of a defence. She was with other people. Can you find someone to say they forced her to do it? Threatened her? You think of something. You'll find someone else to take the blame. That's your special subject, isn't it, Chippy?'

He still looked up at me and said quietly, 'I ought to get you killed, Terry.'

'That wouldn't do you any good.' I managed to sound cheerful. 'She'll tell the story in court anyway. So you just think of a way of helping her out. Think about it, Chippy.'

I left him then. He did think about it, and he found a way out which was no help to Lucy. No help at all.

216

33

EXTRACT FROM THE MINUTES OF THE COUNCIL, SOCIAL CARERS, REFORMERS AND PRAECEPTORS

Special meeting held at SCRAP offices, King's Cross

Present:

GWENDOLEN GERDON, Executive Director (ED)
LADY DOUGHBERRY, representing the Bunyan Society for Prison Reform
PROFESSOR MAXWELL HEATHERINGTON, Reader in Criminology at the University of East Surrey
CAMPBELL DYSON, Chair of Dyson Soft Furnishing
IVY SINCLAIR, BBC *Today* programme
PETER BETHELL, partner in the firm of Bethell, Sherman and Pensotti, Solicitors
THE REV. HARVEY TYLER, Rector, St Barnabas, King's Cross
ALEX MARKBY, representing the Probation Service

Gwendolen Gerdon (the ED) read out the letter received from the chair, Leonard McGrath.

To the members of the council of SCRAP. My doctors have informed me that the British climate is seriously damaging my health and it is essential that I move to a place abroad where I can enjoy the benefits of sunshine and warmth. To delay my departure would have risked further damage to the condition of my chest and lungs, so I'm sorry to say that I shall be out of the country when the council receives this letter.

I would like to add that it has been a pleasure and an honour to have been chair of SCRAP. I wish you all success under your new chair. Carry on with the good work!

Yours sincerely,
Leonard McGrath

The Rev. Harvey Tyler asked if Leonard McGrath had given any address of his residence abroad so that messages of sympathy and gratitude might be sent to him. The ED told the meeting that she had no information as to the whereabouts of our former chair, except it was clearly 'a place in the sun'. She had made enquiries and discovered that his maisonette in Connaught Square was 'up for sale'.

A motion was proposed by the Rev. Harvey Tyler and seconded by Lady Doughberry thanking Leonard McGrath for his inspirational leadership of SCRAP, to be sent to him as soon as the ED discovered his address.

Professor Maxwell Heatherington suggested that the meeting should proceed to elect a new chair. Various names were suggested, including Princess Anne, Mr Terry Wogan and Dame Judi Dench.

After further discussion, Peter Bethell said that we need look no further than this room to find an excellent chair, one with huge experience of the problems of prison and prisoners, and he proposed Mr Alex Markby and he was seconded by Mr Campbell Dyson. Mr Markby said he was taken aback at being offered such a great honour and his first instinct was to refuse, but after further thought he was persuaded that his long experience of the reform of ex-prisoners and finding them a useful place in society would be of value in a chair. 'Leonard McGrath,' he said, 'would be a hard act to follow, but I can only do my best.'

The proposal to elect Mr Alex Markby chair was carried nem. con. There being no further business, the ED declared the special meeting closed and tea was served early at 3.30 p.m.

34

Time passed in Holloway, where the days were all the same: get up, breakfast, laundry, dinner, more work, association and locked up for the night. Martine was getting nearer to having her baby and I began to tell the passing of time by the progress of her pregnancy. Otherwise, we were killing time waiting for the days to pass, in my case until the date of my trial, when I expected to find out how much more time I would have to kill.

When Terry came a few more times to visit, he looked at me sadly as though I hadn't done what I did to be close to him, and now I felt he was getting further and further away from me. Finally we didn't seem to have much to say to each other. All he wanted to talk about was how well he got on with Mr Markby, his probation officer, now chairman of SCRAP since that Chippy McGrath had done a runner.

He told me that he'd threatened to expose Chippy unless he admitted he'd forced me to steal the picture. That was why Chippy left the country. I told him it was a daft idea anyway and no one forced me to steal the picture, which had been entirely my Great Idea. After that we found even less to say to each other.

Persephone Smith-Aldeney visited me from Aldershot and showed me one of the tabloids with a huge article by Robin Thirkell under the screaming headline 'Bishop's Daughter Invaded My Home Because I'd Ended Our Torrid Love Affair'. She said the tabloid in question was delighted with Robin's article, so they'd offered him a weekly restaurant column and 'good money'.

I thought at least someone had profited from this mess, although it did seem that some tabloids would believe anything.

So the days passed, working in the laundry, waiting for Martine's baby and having Miss Wickstead, the screw, watching my every movement, hoping that I might get 'prison bent' in her direction. Then they told me I had another visitor and, surprise, surprise, who should I find sitting at the table in the visitors' centre but my usually not very talkative mother.

Sylvia had scrubbed up for the occasion. Her hair looked as though it had been done specially and she'd brought me a box of chocolates, in the way she did when she visited me at school.

'What an extraordinary place!' She looked round at the tables where girls were meeting their husbands or boyfriends and bored children were longing for the visits to end.

'Yes,' I said. 'It's very extraordinary.'

'I've never been in a prison before.' Strangely enough, Sylvia looked as though she regretted it.

'No, Mum, I don't suppose you have.'

'It's a new experience for you too, is it, Lucy?' My mother seemed to have only the vaguest idea of what I'd been doing since I left home.

'Yes, Mum. A completely new experience.'

'And it's not too bad in here?'

'No, it's not too bad. A bit better than St Swithin's. At least we have a heated swimming pool. Oh, and a ghost.'

'What ghost?'

'Ruth Ellis. They hung her because she shot her

lover.'

'Oh, I remember. They shouldn't have done that.' My mother looked vaguely into the middle distance.

'No, they shouldn't.'

'Have you ever seen this ghost?'

'Once or twice I thought I saw her, yes.'

'Well, let's hope you did.'

'Why?'

'Not much point in being a ghost if nobody sees you.' My mother giggled as though she had said something extremely funny. I wondered how long it was since we last sat down to have a talk to each other.

'You know I met your father in Ronnie Scott's?'

'Yes, Mum. I did know.'

Whenever Dad was writing a sermon the palace still echoed to Dizzie Gillespie and Charlie Parker, Sidney Bechet and Muddy Waters. I knew he'd met Mum at a jazz club.

'When I took him home my parents were so pleased because they'd found out he was a vicar with bishop potential. I only liked him because I found him sexually attractive.'

This was wonderful. The prison atmosphere was clearly bringing the best out in my mother. I had never thought that we would have this conversation.

'So you had a great sex life, did you, Mum?' This question, which I wouldn't have dreamed of asking my mother before this prison visit, didn't seem to worry her at all.

'Oh yes. Two or three times a night. Even more some Sundays! When he was a vicar. That was when you were conceived and all that sort of thing.

222

It was when he was a bishop that the trouble started. I suppose I shouldn't be telling you all this.'

'What was the trouble then, Mum?' She really didn't seem to mind telling me.

'God.'

I looked round the room. Children were bored, eating sweets from the prison shop. Couples could no longer think of anything to say to each other. The screws were looking on and Mum was unexpectedly pouring out her heart.

'How did God come into it?'

'Well, he didn't really. Not when Robert was a vicar. In those days he seemed to take God for granted. But as soon as he became a bishop—I don't know, I suppose because it was a step up and Robert felt responsible for God and treated him more as an equal. Anyway, he began to find fault with him or question anything he did. Of course, it's got a lot worse since President Bush. He can't understand how God would have anything to do with the man.'

'But how did this affect you?' I knew a lot about Robert's troubles, but now my mum was opening her heart to me.

'Well, he seemed to think much more about God than he did about me. And then he got so keen on gay and lesbian marriages.'

'You think that was a bad thing?'

'Not in itself. I mean, I don't give tuppence for what they do among themselves. It's their world and they're welcome to it. But Robert seemed so interested in their sex lives that he forgot all about ours.'

'I'm sorry.'

'So am I. And I'm afraid there's even worse news ahead. Will London's about to retire. He's got something wrong with his brain. Robert's been strongly recommended as his successor.'

'Bishop of London?'

'Of course the idea's ridiculous, but Robert's enormously excited about it. It'll be very controversial and there are already letters against him in the *Daily Telegraph*. Robert likes that, having letters against him in the *Daily Telegraph*.'

'Well, who's for him then?'

'The Prime Minister apparently thinks he's a "modernizer" who's prepared to draw a line under the old conservative Church of England. Oh, I do so hope it never happens.'

'Why, exactly?'

'I've got used to the palace at Aldershot. I know the stairs. I love the peculiar little scullery. I don't want to go to London, Lucy. I prayed to God it doesn't happen.'

'Well then . . .'

'But I'm not sure he was listening. I'm not sure he listens to people's prayers any more. Perhaps he's had enough of it by now. All the same, Lucy, what I can say to you is, don't ever marry a man with bishop potential.'

'Don't worry. My boyfriend's a burglar.'

'I know, dear. Your father told me.'

'Even though he may be my ex-boyfriend now.'

'Don't worry, Lucy. You're not to worry. You've done something with your life.'

'Have I?'

'You've had an extraordinary experience. I never had an extraordinary experience and I don't suppose I ever shall.'

Then it was time for her to go. When we stood up I put my arms round her and told her that I loved her. She left me then, smiling sweetly to herself.

*　　　*　　　*

The visit from my mother went well, but the same couldn't be said of my visits from Terry. He had told me about Chippy vanishing from the scene to an unknown address somewhere in the world. He reported that the maisonette was empty and up for sale, the awful secretary had gone off, presumably with Chippy, and Screwtop and Ozzy Desmond were nowhere to be found. He kept telling me he was going straight and divided his time between chatting up his probation officer and helping out in various restaurants. He also said that I shouldn't get too close to the girls in my room as they were probably all reoffenders and I might end up by being as bad as them.

This attitude of Terry's to my girl friends got under my skin more than a bit, particularly as the great excitement for all of us was the arrival of Martine's baby. I told him I thought it would be better if he didn't visit me any more, at least until I could get my head straight. He seemed quite startled when I told him that, but he just muttered, 'OK then,' and left the visitors' room. I didn't see him after that, not for a long time.

Martine had been moved into the mother and baby unit in a four-bedded room with three other mothers-to-be. Then we heard that she'd been moved to the labour ward of the Whittington Hospital, where she could stay for no more than

225

seventy-two hours. But that was long enough to produce what she came back with. We got passes to see him and of course everyone agreed with Martine that he was just the most marvellous baby that had ever been born in the world. His name was Nicholas, but she called him Nick—which I thought was an appropriate name if he grew up pinching things like his mother. But of course I never said that.

Martine was now in a single room with Nick. She wasn't locked up at night, but she couldn't leave the room without permission. So we marked the passage of time by Nick's various achievements. We remembered the first day he smiled, when he started on solid food, when he sat up and we had a big day of celebration when he crawled.

Behind all these achievements, though, there was a horrible worry for Martine. Each step forward brought Nick nearer to being nine months old, when he and his mother would have to be parted. And if Martine had no home to send him to, he would be put into care and it would be goodbye to Nicholas.

Well, she hadn't got a home. Martine's mother was a crack-head who'd only left Holloway a month or so before we arrived. Of course she had friends, but they were a drifting population of airheads and regular offenders. There seemed to be no one to look after Nick until Martine finished her sentence. I have to say that this worried me more than thoughts of my coming appearance at the Old Bailey.

Of course I got another visit from Peter Bethell, who brought with him a youngish, tallish and enthusiastic man who seemed to find everything he said himself irresistibly funny, although I noticed he never laughed when Mr Bethell made anything at all like a joke.

'We've briefed Mr Frobisher for your case, Lucy,' Mr Bethell told me. 'I used him the other day in the Court of Appeal.'

'I managed to tie them up in knots on the quality of criminal intent.' Mr Frobisher laughed heartily.

'So you did, Mr Frobisher. You had the Lords Justice of the Court of Appeal "appealing" for mercy.' Mr Bethell, certainly in a good mood, laughed loudly, but Mr Frobisher didn't crack a smile.

'We thought a brilliant young junior was better than a QC in your particular case,' Mr Bethell said. 'And we didn't want to put the bishop to unnecessary expense.'

'I don't want my father put to any expense at all.'

'Mr George Frobisher,' Peter Bethell assured me, 'can see further through a brick wall than most of us. He says it's not too late.'

'Too late for what?' I asked them.

'For you to say it was all a joke on your old friend Robin Thirkell.'

'Just a bit of a prank.' Mr Frobisher seemed overcome by laughter. 'We'll get a judge with a sense of humour. They do exist, you know.'

'Mr Frobisher knows his judges,' Peter Bethell assured me.

'We want the sort of chap who was capable of sewing up his best friend's trouser legs, or putting a ferret in his bed in college days.'

Mr Bethell smiled vaguely. I was sure he didn't know of any judge who'd put a ferret in his best friend's bed at any time of his life. Honestly, I needed to put an end to this nonsense. 'It wasn't a joke,' I said, 'or a prank and I didn't sew up anyone's trousers. It was deadly serious.'

'I told you.' Peter Bethell turned to the barrister sadly. 'It was deadly serious. She was deeply in love at the time.'

'I can't see why being deeply in love should make you go around stealing people's artworks.' Saying this made Mr Frobisher laugh again and Peter Bethell joined in obediently.

'Then you can't understand my case at all,' I told them. 'I'm just going to say I'm guilty and go back to prison. Oh, perhaps now you're both here you could think of a legal way of stopping Martine having her child taken away from her when he's nine months old.'

But they couldn't. They weren't any use at all. Either of them.

35

Time passed. I'd stopped visiting Holloway, quite honestly because Lucy didn't want to see me again. Talk about attitude! Hers seemed to have changed from love, real proper love, to what you might call irritation. Just because I wanted to be what she once wanted me to be. Now she was angry because I wanted the odd GCSE or A level or to go straight.

Of course I'd had girlfriends before, plenty of them, and I had no trouble at all understanding what they wanted. A good time, of course, plenty of drinks and the occasional illegal substance, and if you're suddenly flush with money a couple of weeks on the Costa del Crime. I'd been happy to oblige and the truth is that I'd never been given the push before. It may be a bit arrogant of me to say this but it always either fizzled out or I was the one who decided we weren't best suited.

It was different with Lucy. Come to think of it, everything was different with Lucy. If I was to be honest about it I'd have to admit that it was because I cared for her more than I'd ever cared for any of the others. So I suppose that's why I felt so badly about it. If she didn't fancy me any more, for whatever reason, I wasn't going to turn up in the Holloway visitors' room just for the pleasure of discovering that my girlfriend had got bored with me and couldn't wait for the visit to be over.

As she'd ended our relationship I thought it wasn't fair to stay on in her flat in the Notting Hill area, so I locked it up and moved away. I'll admit I borrowed some of her books I needed for studying. I found myself a room above a Japanese restaurant down the Goldhawk Road. Never mind I had to share a bathroom with the head sushi cook. He was spotlessly clean and would send me up a few bits of sushi when he thought I looked hungry. It was a long way from cooking up a rack of lamb for Lucy in her flat, but let's say I survived on it and it was a lot better than being locked up inside like she was.

I went over to the Brummell Club in the days when I still had a bit of money stored up against my retirement and one night there, drinking at the bar as large as life and twice as natural, was Screwtop. I sat down beside him, allowed him to order me a large vodka on the rocks and then I accused him of leading the scam which was so stupidly organized that it had landed my ex-girlfriend inside.

'She hasn't told you that, has she?' Screwtop looked seriously worried.

'No.' I did my best to reassure him, although to be honest he wasn't wanting reassuring. 'She hasn't told anyone. When I found out she was with a couple of pros who left her in her hour of need, I thought one of them must have been you.'

'She's a good girl.' Screwtop looked horribly self-satisfied.

'She's not a good girl,' I told him. 'And that's why she's in Holloway Prison.'

'And what about you?' Screwtop wasn't worried about Lucy now he'd found out she wasn't going to shop him. 'You done any good jobs lately?'

'Helped out in the kitchens of Il Deliciosa in Westbourne Terrace.'

'You mean you're going legitimate?'

'That's what I mean.'

'That can't be very profitable.'

'No, it isn't. But it gives me time to study. I hope to get a few more qualifications. What about you?'

'Been abroad.' Screwtop picked up his glass and looked very pleased with himself. 'Came back to clear up a few things and then I'll be away again.'

'Like Chippy?' it occurred to me to ask him.

'Yes. Very like Chippy.' Screwtop gulped down his drink and said, 'We may be working together again. Somewhere you can make money by the bucketful.'

'Oh yes?' I tried not to sound too interested. 'Where's that exactly?'

Screwtop wouldn't have told me so much if he'd been entirely sober. As it was he leaned forward and, with his vodka breath, whispered one word in my ear: 'Iraq.'

Screwtop left the Brummell then and I never saw or spoke to him or Chippy again.

*   *   *

Like I say, time passed. Thanks to Mr Markby I got lessons through the post. It wasn't the Milton book I had to read but one about animals talking about politics and one from America about a halfwitted man. I wrote down my thoughts about these books and posted them off, and got quite encouraging letters back. When it came to Christmas, Mr Markby invited me to lunch at his home in Enfield.

So I sat round a table with Mr and Mrs Markby and her sister and her sister's husband and one or two more friends and someone who worked in the Prison Inspectors Office and we all put on paper crowns out of the crackers and Mr Markby read out the jokes, which as far as I was concerned didn't raise a laugh at all. I was mainly worried about Mr Markby's little dog, who seemed dead set on eating the ends of my trousers. Mr Markby told them all that we'd first met when I was in prison and they looked at me, particularly the young Markby, Simon, with a sort of respect as though he'd told them that I'd swum the Channel or crossed the Arctic with dogs.

After a few glasses of port and a few more crackers, Mr Markby told them all how he'd delayed my parole.

'I thought he gave me all the right answers but he didn't mean them. Now I know he's changed. He's particularly anxious to stop a friend getting into more trouble. Terry's a fine example of the way that prison works.'

Mr Markby, whose paper crown was now a bit askew, raised his glass to that, and I didn't argue. The fact that I'd come a long way from my sort of home with my Aunt Dot and Uncle Arthur, who was continually away, to the Markbys' Christmas dinner was, I thought, a bit of an achievement. So I told them that I was grateful for what Mr Markby had done for me, and I suppose I meant it. All the same, I went and got a bit drunk in a pub down the Goldhawk Road the next night. All I'd done to keep my friend out of trouble had got me no further than Christmas dinner with the Markby family.

*　　　*　　　*

232

More time passed and I found myself in another public gallery, this time in Number 2 Court down at the Old Bailey. Mr Bethell had told me the date of Lucy's trial, and that it was going to be a pretty short story as my ex-girlfriend had made up her mind to plead guilty and 'Counsel and I couldn't persuade her to make a fight of it.' Lucky for Lucy it wasn't Judge Bullingham, who had seen me off for four years the last time I visited the Old Bailey. It was a small, neat, pocket-sized judge called Springer. From the way he handed out prison sentences in the guilty cases before Lucy he seemed a polite sort of person who always said, 'The least sentence I could possibly pass in this case is . . .' unlike fucking Bullingham, who not only gave out what seemed to be the maximum but was bloody rude with it.

When the turn came to 'Bring up Purefoy' I craned forward in my seat, to see Lucy looking round the court as though she was already bored with the whole proceedings. Whether that was what she really felt or she was just putting on an act I didn't honestly know, because I'd got so far out of touch with Lucy's feelings. She had a sort of uninterested look on her face, and didn't even give a glance up to the public gallery although I was staring at her so hard that I thought she must have felt it, however far away she was.

The prosecution told the story you've heard often enough of the stolen picture and then the brief Mr Bethell had landed Lucy with got up to make his speech. He was a tall, lanky sort of person who didn't seem able to control his giggles.

'Your Lordship,' he started off merrily enough,

233

'may well feel there is a good deal of comedy about this particular case.'

'I find it difficult, Mr Frobisher,' the judge told Lucy's brief, 'to see a comic side to burglary.' This ought to have given the lanky brief a fair warning, but he went on doing his stand-up stuff.

'The whole business was such a disaster that I must say I find the facts as they have been outlined by my learned friend who appears for the prosecution most amusing.'

'Do you indeed?' Mr Justice Springer looked determined to be serious. 'May I remind you that the purpose of the Central Criminal Court in England is not to amuse you, Mr Frobisher.'

Even this didn't wipe the grin off Mr Frobisher's face. 'She undertook this picture-stealing operation having first alerted Detective Sergeant Macdonald, who was able to guess that she had some such ridiculous enterprise in mind.'

'Are you suggesting, Mr Frobisher,' the judge asked, 'the inefficiency of a burglar should lead to a shorter sentence?'

'Let me put it this way, My Lord,' Mr Frobisher invited the judge to enjoy what he clearly thought was an excellent joke, 'Lucy Purefoy was helping the police with their enquiries.'

The judge didn't join in the fun. He didn't even crack a smile as he said, 'It seems clear that she arrived at the scene with some more professional accomplices and she has refused to name them. That was hardly helping the police with their enquiries, was it, Mr Frobisher?'

'May I remind Your Lordship that they had disappeared before my client started to remove the picture?'

'I am also reminded that they disappeared with a selection of Mr Thirkell's silver cutlery. Have you any further submissions to make, Mr Frobisher?'

Mr Frobisher hadn't. He sat down with his jokey smile turned to a look of some anxiety.

Lucy, who had been sitting unsmiling through all Mr Frobisher's jokes, was told to stand. She did, and I can still hear what the judge said to her now. There wasn't a single laugh in it.

'Lucinda Purefoy, you entered a house by night and were caught in the act of stealing a very valuable picture from a friend to whom you stood, to some extent, in a position of trust. I utterly reject Mr Frobisher's speech in mitigation. Although ill-conceived, it has done nothing actually to increase the sentence I am about to pass. You will go to prison for three years. Take her down.'

I thought that Lucy would at least glance up at the public gallery to see if I was there before she went, but she did nothing of the sort. She went towards the steps down from the dock to the cells as though she couldn't wait to get away from the whole courtroom, including me if I happened to be there. I didn't see her again for some considerable time.

36

After my so-called trial, Mr Bethell and that ass of a barrister he found for me came down to the cells, I suppose to say goodbye. They were both angry with the judge, not because of my sentence, but because he'd ticked Mr Frobisher off for his so-called comic speech. 'Speaking to learned counsel like that in public and in front of the client too. It's not what we expect of Her Majesty's judges,' was what Mr Bethell said.

'I think my back is broad enough to bear anything Judge Stringer might have to throw at me.' The jokey Frobisher was still grinning and apparently felt that he'd been very brave in court, at which point Mr Bethell seemed to feel that, although I hadn't been treated so badly by the judge as his barrister had, I might need a little consoling too. 'Three years doesn't really mean three years,' he told me.

It turned out that I'd get a third off for good behaviour and that the time I'd been in prison waiting for a trial would be taken into consideration, so I should be out early next year.

'So that's not so bad then, is it?'

I had a strange feeling, a sort of dread at being let out to join the world again, but I said nothing and Mr Bethell changed the subject.

'I told your friend Terry Keegan the date of the trial. He was there in the public gallery. Did you notice him?'

'No,' I told him. 'I didn't notice him at all.'

And so far as I could tell, I was never going to

notice him again. Not so long as I lived.

*   *   *

I should have made it clear that my dad was visiting me all the time I was in Holloway. He was lovely of course and kind, but so anxious not to appear what he called 'judgemental' that he did not have anything really valuable to say. In fact at first I had to spend the time trying to cheer him up and comforting him because of the mess he'd undoubtedly made of my bail application when he asked the DPP's man if he enjoyed prawn cocktail.

'I'm still not altogether sure about *why* you wanted to take Robin's picture,' he said when we finally got round to a discussion of the subject.

'You could say I did it for love.'

'Indeed? People do strange things for love. Very strange things indeed.' And then he returned to the subject that really excited him, his possible promotion to be Bishop of London. 'It's caused a great deal of controversy. In the newspapers, on the radio and television. It's regarded as one of the most controversial issues that's faced the Church for generations.' He was glowing with pride. 'I think Canterbury's for it, he doesn't want to go down in history as an old fuddy-duddy.'

'Mum's against it,' I reminded him. 'She loves the scullery in the palace at Aldershot.'

'Who knows? We may find our own better scullery in London. The progress of the spiritual life can't be entirely decided on the convenience of sculleries.'

'She thinks it'd be too much of an upheaval.'

'The history of our Church is one of continual

upheavals.'

'Yes. But Mum doesn't feel she has to be part of the history of the Church. I mean, she's not going to be Bishop of London, is she?'

'That's true.' Robert was giving this new thought fair consideration. 'It's very true.'

'She's praying to God you don't get the job.'

'Is she really? She's not the only one, I can tell you.' My dad seemed flattered by this attention. 'There is a whole new movement within the General Synod opposing my promotion! Can you imagine that? They call themselves the Play It by the Rules Movement. They're dead against gay marriages and homosexual priests and one-parent families. They say . . .' now Robert was chuckling with delight at the idea of a new controversy, 'that the Church of England has certain age-old, always respected rules, like sport. I mean, you mustn't punch below the belt in boxing, you mustn't trip people up in football, you mustn't bowl at their bodies in cricket. So you must play it by the rules in Church. No same-sex marriages etc., no gay clerics, because that would be hitting below the belt. I tell you, Lucy, the movement's attracting a lot of supporters and they'll make quite a lot of fuss at the synod. Of course, you'll never guess who their leader is.'

I told him I never would.

'Who else but my former chaplain, Timbo. Of course he knows all about sport.'

Timbo, I remembered, who tried to start a fight with Terry and, instead, started another chapter in our lives. Timbo, who had emerged once more from his corner to fight my dad. I didn't wish him any luck at all. 'How are you going to deal with

238

him?' I wanted to know.

'By trying to point out that there are considerable differences between religion and cricket. That's quite a hard point to get across in England.' And having thought of this line, my dad hurried off to give it to the press.

*　　　*　　　*

I remembered Robert coming over after I'd been sentenced and looking at me sadly and asking, I thought a bit pathetically, if there was anything he could do to help. So, rather to his surprise, I said there was.

Then I told him about Martine's baby, Nick, who we all loved, and was going to be taken away from her when he reached nine months old.

'What can I do about it?' Dad asked with what I thought was rather a helpless smile.

'I don't know. Do some knee work. Get God on the case. Put it in your friendly newspapers. Ring the Prime Minister, get the Archbishop of Canterbury to say it's a major sin to part mothers from their children.'

Dad considered this and then his eyes lit up. 'Suffer the little children,' he said. 'It might make quite an effective "Thought for the Day" on Radio 4.'

'Do it,' I told him. 'Do it as soon as you can.'

Nick had just reached his nine-month birthday when they came to take him away. Martine couldn't satisfy them she had a respectable home for him. Her mother was rubbish and back on drugs, her father was unknown and her friends not particularly reliable. They didn't hang about, the so-called Welfare Services didn't. They came and took Nick away to put him in so-called 'care'.

Martine came back to our dorm from the mother and baby unit when she lost her child. It was as though Nick had died on her. She didn't say much about it, but at night she cried. She kept us awake with her crying but no one complained of that because by now we understood her. We'd loved Nick too, but of course not in the way Martine had. I was glad I was still in Holloway to help her.

We were all on Martine's side and we all hated the Welfare Services for what they had done more than we hated the police or the judges or even 'Hell' the screw, who was continually pestering me with her attentions although I tried to make it clear to her that I had no intention of becoming 'prison bent' or bent in any way at all.

So we fed Martine with hopes that she'd manage to find Nick when she got out and get him back because she'd get a job and make a good home for him which even the welfare people would approve of. She presumably didn't believe this any more, deep down, than we did. But it kept her from crying so much at night, except on important days, like when Nick would have been one year old and she had no idea where he was or what had happened to him.

Of course, I had alerted Robert when it was about to happen and he did a 'Thought for the Day' about it which someone heard on the radio and said it was very good and effective. It made absolutely no difference at all.

37

They certainly don't make giving up crime easy. Mr Markby had some idea of me ending up in a university, but no university was going to take me with a criminal record. There were better jobs going than helping out in the Notting Hill restaurants, but I had to fill in a CV and Mr Markby told me then I had to mention all my form because they'd check with the police records anyway and the result was that I never got any of the jobs concerned.

When Lucy stepped down from the dock and never even looked at me, I knew it was well and truly over. I supposed she'd come out of Holloway eventually and go back to her dad's palace or somewhere like it, and maybe end up by marrying that old boyfriend Tom she dumped what seemed like years and years ago. So I decided to forget her, but it was hard. Just as hard, it seemed, as getting into university or a decent job. But I needed a new life, that was what I needed.

One of the restaurants I worked in was called Il Deliciosa in Westbourne Terrace. No one who worked or cooked in it was at all Italian. Alysia was the manageress, a tall dark-haired woman with greenish eyes that were always wide open in surprise at finding a dirty ashtray or unswept crumbs on any of the Deliciosa's tables. She definitely ruled the place, and most of them in the kitchen and all the girls who did temporary waitressing to pay their university debts were scared stiff of her. I wasn't scared because I got the feeling she fancied me, and I thought she wasn't so bad with all the flashing eyes and dark hair she pushed away from her face when she was really angry. One day when we were in the kitchen she said, 'We ought to have a date. I'll take you dancing.' It seemed a sort of order, like, 'We'll do Italian meatballs or stuffed aubergines for the special tonight.' So I agreed to go dancing with her on a Monday night when the restaurant was closed.

'I'm going to take you real dancing,' she told me, 'not this present-day rubbish where you just wiggle your bottom and wave your fists in the air. None of that at all. Strictly ballroom. You'll be able to do that, won't you, Terry?' At that time I had no idea how strict the ballroom was going to be.

We met at a bar in Shepherd's Bush. Alysia had high-heeled shoes and a skirt full of pleats and she was clearly excited. I was wearing the only suit I'd been able to save up for. Alysia took me to a place called the Palais Glide off Hammersmith Broadway. At first I looked round in astonishment. There was a small three-piece band playing tunes I didn't recognize and couples like us in suits and pleated skirts with their arms round each other's waists and holding up each other's hands so that they were in close contact gliding, or sliding or sometimes just walking round the floor. I suppose my Aunt Dot and my Uncle Arthur might have danced like that some time, but it wasn't anything I knew about.

Before I could draw breath, Alysia had grabbed me and had me joining in. She was going backwards but she led me definitely. She

242

occasionally leaned right back and made me lean over her. Then she pushed me back and leaned over me. She called out for me to do something called 'chassé at the bends', and I gave a little hop because I had no idea what she was talking about. We went on dancing for what seemed like hours. I was pulled this way and that way, I was told to lean over and lean back by Alysia, her eyes shining with excitement.

There was no licence in the Palais Glide so from time to time we stopped for a Diet Coke. In one of these rest periods Alysia asked me where I lived and I told her over the sushi restaurant. It was then she asked me if I had a big bed.

Well, by now you'll have guessed what happened, and at midnight Alysia got out of my bed, which isn't as big as all that, and started to put on her clothes. When I asked her what the matter was she told me. 'You're no good at ballroom and when were in bed you were thinking of someone else. Go on! Admit it.'

I should never have done it, I suppose, but I'd got in a way of trying to be honest. 'All right,' I said, 'quite honestly I did sometimes think of her.'

'Sometimes! Who was she anyway?'

'Someone I knew. She said she wanted to do some good in the world when I met her.'

'Do some good!' The green eyes were very angry, which I knew was only to be expected. 'How very disgusting! What's she doing? Feeding the starving Africans, I suppose. What is she, a missionary or something?'

'No, she's in Holloway Prison. She's doing three years for burglary.'

'That's not true!' Alysia couldn't believe it.

'Quite true.'

'How disgusting!' She was buttoning up as though she couldn't wait to get out of my place.

'Not too disgusting. I think she wanted to be like me.'

'Well, you haven't done three years for burglary, have you?'

'Not really. The last time I was inside I got four.'

She was still then, very still. Then she said, 'Does Geoffrey know that?' Geoffrey Parsons being the owner of Il Deliciosa.

'I don't think so.'

'You never told him?'

'No.'

'Why not?'

'It was one of the jobs where I didn't have to produce my CV. That's why I took it.'

She was out of my place like a flash. It was the end of our conversation and the end of my job too, because Mr Geoffrey Parsons gave me the sack. I knew I had no one to blame but myself. I should never have gone dancing.

*   *   *

'I was trying to be honest,' I told Mr Markby when I next saw him. 'That was a mistake, wasn't it?'

'Not necessarily. Honesty's quite important in our sort of work.'

'You think I should be a probation officer?'

'You might be quite a good probation officer with all your experience of prisons. Unfortunately it seems that your convictions make it impossible. Though I have thought of one job,' he was actually smiling at me, 'where you might just possibly be

244

rather successful.'

'What's that?' I wasn't expecting very much.

'I just have to consult a few people,' he said. 'I'll tell you later.'

38

It was hard work saying goodbye.

I really didn't want to leave them, particularly as it now seemed I was going out into a world where I found it hard to remember what to do exactly. It was a question I hardly dared ask, let alone answer. Anyway, the goodbyes came first.

Devira gave me a handkerchief she had embroidered for me and held her hands together in what I supposed was a sort of blessing when I left her to her life sentence.

I promised Martine that I'd set about finding out where they'd put Nick, though I'd no idea how to do that or even where to begin. Of course I promised to write to her. 'Hell' the screw told me about all the good times I'd missed and the privileges I'd done without by not being a bit more cooperative, and I allowed her a kiss, strictly confined to my left cheekbone.

They were a bit slow in the office that morning and it took a long time to give me back the clothes I wore when I was arrested—the jeans and sweater and trainers which I'd put on to climb into Robin Thirkell's house for the sake of excitement and the picture of Madame Bonnard drying herself after the bath.

And then the screw with the big jangling bunch of keys unlocked the door and let me out into an uncertain future with a travel warrant and £46.75 and not too much of a prospect of getting back to work in the advertising business.

It was a grey, damp morning early in the year

and the traffic outside Holloway, after the calm silences of prison, sounded almost unbearably loud. I only had time for one quick look round before I saw him. I don't know why but I found it irritating that he hadn't changed at all. He still had dark curly hair and he'd fixed on a determinedly cheerful smile as he bore down on me.

And then he said, as though it was a joke, 'You must be Lucy Purefoy.'

'What the hell,' I asked him, 'do you think you're talking about, you know damn well who I am.'

'But you don't know who I am.' He gave me the news as though he thought he was giving me good news. 'I'm your praeceptor.'

'My *what*?'

'Of course you know what a praeceptor is, you did Latin at school. It means I'm your guide, philosopher and friend, although Mr Markby warned me not to get too friendly, at least at first. I'm here to see you get a job, settle you back in the flat, see you never go inside that place again.'

'Well, don't bother!' I felt I had to tell him. 'Anyway, what's Mr Markby got to do with it?'

'He's the new chair of SCRAP. I told you he got the job after Chippy did a great big runner. I was having a hard time getting a job on account of my record so he found me one at SCRAP. Paid praeceptor in charge of special cases. You're one of them.'

'I'm certainly not!'

'I'm only here to help you.'

'Then go back to the Scrubs and help some other poor bugger. I don't need your help now, Terry.'

247

'That's what they always say.'

'All right. I've said it.'

'You know perfectly well 85 per cent of prisoners reoffend within two years of their release. I'm going to help you stop that habit of stealing things.'

'You mean you're here to reform me?'

'You could say that, yes.'

'Well, you can fuck off then.'

Just as he had once long ago, Terry looked surprised and pained as I said that. I know what he meant. Women weren't meant to swear or do the burglaries, those were jobs for men. Terry's male chauvinism was coming out again. This time, though, he was making a bit of an effort to control it.

'All right then,' he said, 'if that's the way you feel, that's all right. All I'd suggest is we do one thing together. If you don't want to see me after that, I'll piss off and leave you alone.'

'One thing?' I was extremely doubtful. Did he mean sex? What was this one thing?

'I got up early to get here on time and I missed breakfast. Are you feeling hungry? What would you say to a burger?'

The rain was falling steadily and the traffic was even noisier. A crowd of children were running down the pavement on their way to school. I was facing a day with nothing much to do. Also I suddenly felt, having been too busy saying goodbye to eat breakfast, unexpectedly hungry. I looked at Terry and for another inexplicable moment I didn't want to disappoint him.

'All right,' I said. 'If you mean just one hamburger.'

'Just one,' he promised. 'But a whopper!'

There was a taxi passing and SCRAP must have been paying expenses because he stopped it.

And that's where this story begins again.

39

So there I was, waiting outside the gates of Holloway Prison quite early one grey morning with the rain coming down. And then I saw her coming towards me, not much changed, I have to admit, but a bit paler. People coming out of prison always seem paler than those of us on the outside, but still her, still how she was when she left the dock after she turned her back on me. I knew it wasn't going to be easy. As Mr Markby said, 'To be honest, our job's never easy.' She didn't look at all pleased to see me.

'You must be Lucy Purefoy,' I said. I thought she might see the joke. I thought she might remember how she greeted me when she was waiting for me outside the Scrubs what seemed like all those years ago. She either didn't see it or wasn't in the mood for laughter. 'You know damn well who I am,' was what she said.

Then I explained to her about Mr Markby. How he'd given me the job at SCRAP and got me to be paid wages so I could give all my time to it and not be tempted to reoffend. So I'd tried to help a collection of poor old sods and cocky youths who came out of prison with nothing much provided for them. And then he told me he had this in mind for me, to take Lucy on as a special case. He was impressed by my determination to cure her of the criminal habits she'd got herself into. Well, I told her I was the praeceptor now, her guide, philosopher and friend.

You know, she didn't take it well. But I suppose,

to be honest, I didn't take it well when she said she was going to get me to go straight when we first met outside the Scrubs. But so much had happened between us since then that I sort of hoped she'd have been thinking about that and changed her attitude.

No way, in fact no way at all. She said she didn't need my help. Then she actually asked if I planned to reform her. I had to admit that she could say that. It was then she told me to fuck off. It's true I didn't like hearing her say that, just as I don't like the idea of women doing serious crimes. It doesn't suit women somehow, at least that's the way I look at it. I still expect women to be feminine, if you know what I mean. I think it suits them better.

But I didn't get anywhere with her. 'Never lose your temper with a client,' Mr Markby had told me. 'Never give him, or her, that particular satisfaction.' I'd gone to all sorts of lectures and meetings at SCRAP, I'd read books and magazines about the aftercare of criminals to help me in my new work, and in particular for the job which had brought me to the gate of Holloway, all to be told to fuck off. This would have made me very angry if I hadn't followed Mr Markby's advice.

So, instead of telling Lucy what I thought of her, I suddenly had a new idea. I told her that if she really felt like that I'd piss off and leave her alone. But I felt we ought to do just one thing together before that was decided on.

Of course she thought I meant sex but I didn't mean that at all. At SCRAP they made it clear that the praeceptor mustn't have sex with the client. Well, not during the reforming process anyway. So, instead of any talk about sex, and remembering

251

how we first met, I told her I hadn't had breakfast, which was nothing but the truth, and if she was at all hungry, what about a hamburger.

She thought about it and I was anxious, much too anxious, about how she'd take to this suggestion. In the end she said, 'If you mean just one hamburger.'

'Just one,' I said. 'But a whopper!'

So there it was. It was a start. I had money for expenses and a taxi was crawling by in the rain so I flicked my fingers and we set off towards Notting Hill and the Burger King. At least we were together.

And that's where this story begins again.

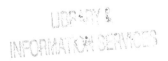

CHIVERS LARGE PRINT —direct—

If you have enjoyed this Large Print book and would like to build up your own collection of Large Print books, please contact

Chivers Large Print Direct

Chivers Large Print Direct offers you a full service:

- Prompt mail order service

- Easy-to-read type

- The very best authors

- Special low prices

For further details either call
Customer Services on (01225) 336552
or write to us at Chivers Large Print Direct,
FREEPOST, Bath BA1 3ZZ

Telephone Orders:
FREEPHONE 08081 72 74 75